ALSO BY ROMAIN GARY

THE COMPANY OF MEN

THE COLORS OF THE DAY

THE ROOTS OF HEAVEN

LADY L.

A NOVEL BY

ROMAIN GARY

SIMON AND SCHUSTER · NEW YORK · 1959

To Lady L.

CHAPTER ONE

The window was open. The bouquet of tulips and roses, against the blue of the sky and the light summer air, reminded her of Matisse, and even the yellow petals falling on the window ledge seemed to arrange themselves gracefully for a master's brush. Lady L. hated yellow and she wondered how the flowers had found their way into the Ming vase. There had been a time when every bouquet in the house had first to be presented to her for inspection and approval.

1

But she was very old now and she was becoming a little detached and indifferent. Then there were the years, before the First World War, when she had kept a Japanese flower artist of the famous Tani School, but he was a little too self-conscious in his effects, his arrangements too premeditated, and during his reign the flowers had lacked freedom. Later she had taken care of them herself, and her gardens both in England and in Italy became perhaps even more famous than her own beauty.

But all this was a long time ago.

She was reclining in her chair, her head resting against the small cushion she had always carried with her on her travels for the last thirty years. She liked the embroidery on the cover, which represented all the beasts united together in the peace of the Garden of Eden. Her hand was resting on her cane. She was looking through the window, beyond the chestnut trees, the ponds, the flower beds, toward the dome of the summer pavilion outlined against the English sky, where the clouds and the pale patches of blue always looked rather like the dresses her granddaughters were wearing—strictly conventional and *comme il faut*. The English sky, she had often thought, lacked emotion. Even at its most rainy and stormy, it lacked drama; it still tried

2

to behave. It was a sky that went well with polite society, with good manners and well-brought-up children. But all she was asking from it now was that it stay there, as a blue and tender background, behind the dome of the summer pavilion, so that she could sit and watch it, smiling a little, for hours at a time. The summer pavilion had been built in somewhat Oriental style and it reminded her of the Bosporus and of the Golden Horn, which she loved so dearly. How often she had wished that Delacroix could have painted the walls of her pavilion. Only his lovely, romantic brush could have done it justice.

I am afraid I am still quite, quite romantic, she thought. She smiled again, almost gaily, at the gold-and-blue cupola showing above the chestnut trees, and then suddenly there were a few tears in her eyes. But this was only because she was so very old. Lady L. was eighty and it was her birthday and she had had hardly any time today to spend in the only company she had kept for so long. The thin, delicate lips still had a certain air of youthfulness. She had always been famous for her ironic wit, but she no longer cared, and so there was no reason left for trying to be either ironic or witty. Young men still talked to her gladly and looked at her with admiration—those, at least, who still loved women. But this was not a century when women were truly loved.

The light of the day played on her face and the marks of age looked merely like a certain tightening of the skin around the bones. Light was kind to her face: they were old friends, and it had always loved beauty. She herself had now no patience with her face. It made her cross. She knew that she was now only, as they put it, "a splendid old lady," and it was quite, quite terrible that after all those years one had had to waste being a lady, one had to put up now with being old as well. Somehow she couldn't quite convince herself that she was eighty, and it seemed to her strange that age was something that should have happened to her. And although she knew that her dark, gay eyes, her delicate nose, firm and both strong and beautiful—they called it, of course, an "aristocratic nose"—and her long neck, perfect in its design, still made every artist long for his crayon, she knew that style was the only thing left to her and that her beauty was now something that could inspire only a painter, not a lover. There is really nothing left of me, she thought, but a few remains—*des restes*.

She was still thinking in French, after fifty-five years in England.

Through the window, to the right, she could see the entrance to the house, with its heavy pillars and the stairs going slowly down toward the lawn like gray waves of lava. She had never liked the house and she had never been able to do anything with it, really. You can never do anything with Vanbrugh, she thought. The house sat heavily on the land: you could almost see it suffer.

A Rolls-Royce came slowly up the driveway and her eldest grandson, James, emerged with his usual pompous and satisfied air. Lady L. watched him with disapproval as he came up the stairs, his briefcase under his arm. James was a director on the board of the Bank of England, and he looked every inch of it.

She hated briefcases, bank directors, family reunions and birthday parties, but, of course, it all had to be—it was all part of her revenge. She looked once more beyond the chestnut trees. That ought to teach you, she thought, waving her cane suddenly at the golden dome. Your son is the present Duke of Glendale. Your eldest grandson, James, is a director of the Bank of England, and if this is not conventional enough for you, then there is Roland, who is a cabinet minister, and Anthony, soon to be a bishop, and Richard, although less successful, is a lieutenant-colonel in the Guards; and there was nothing you hated more than the army, she thought, except, of course, the police and the rich. That ought to teach you.

She could hear the distant voices in the other room and she knew that they were waiting for her, with their beastly birthday cake, wondering what she was doing out there, why she had left them so suddenly saying that she wished to be alone. But of course she was not alone. She was never alone. She gave a last glance through the window and then rose from the chair: she had always hated partings. She didn't have to lean on her cane as she got up. She was still very spry and she could walk for hours, slowly, perhaps, not as she used to, for there was a time, long ago, when she could just walk and walk through all the beauties of the earth, without ever tiring of looking, of listening, of loving. But she had a strong sense of duty and, since her marriage, had always respected the rules of the game, and a birthday was a birthday, even if it was your eightieth one. She thought it very rude of them to make such a fuss over her eightieth birthday, but then no one had any manners nowadays.

And so she rose to join her grandchildren and her great-grandchildren, who were waiting for her. She didn't like them particularly, except the very young one, the little boy—he had *such* lovely dark eyes and fine features and she loved him. The others merely smelled of milk. Her son was rarely in England. "Let's enjoy the world while it's still corrupt" was his last postcard, sent from Persia. All her friends had died young. Gaston, her favorite chef, had been carried off at sixty-seven. People died younger and younger nowadays, she thought. Even pets died younger than they used to. She gave a passing thought to the extraordinary number of pets—dogs, cats, and birds—she had outlived, literally hundreds of them. The life span of a pet was so miserably short; she had given up having them and outliving them long ago—except Old Silly, of course. It was very sad. They hardly began to keep you company, you hardly began to know them and already you had to part. She couldn't bear separations; she even hated to part with objects. She had managed to establish some very happy relationships with objects, and whenever she traveled she always carried hundreds of them with her, which was, of course, considered eccentric in these airplane-conscious, travel-light days.

She opened the door and went into the Green Drawing Room—it was still called "green," which it had been once, but it was almost forty years now that she had redecorated it in white-and-gold Louis XIV *boiseries*. The first to smile pleasantly at her, with hardly a mark of reproach—she had been away from her birthday party for almost an hour and a half—was, of course, Percy, Old Silly, as she had been calling him for God knows how long. She sometimes felt that he was pushing his devotion a little too far and that it was becoming almost inconsiderate. Old Silly or, as the world knew him, Sir Percy Rodiner, the Poet Laureate, had managed to outlive all her other pets and there were times when she almost regretted it. He didn't improve with age, either. As he stood there, with the teacup in his hand, his striped trousers, gold watch chain, stiff high collar and his white mane spreading over his noble head, he reminded her suddenly of that other boy she used to know years ago—Lloyd George. But the Welshman could be witty and impertinent, which Silly could not. Old Percy was perhaps the only writer she had ever known who managed to be truly respectable. That was probably why he had never written a great book. Respectability had always kept his inspiration and his talent back, and thus advanced him socially: the country had bestowed upon him all the honors it could command. But in spite of all these official reassurances, old Percy had never been able to overcome his deep-rooted conviction that writing, particularly poetry, was a frivolous occupation, and he

had always been a little ashamed of himself and longed
to be forgiven. The pathetic thing about him was that
his most famous work was a book of love sonnets,
though how on earth one could hope to know about love
and still expect to remain a gentleman was, for Lady L.,
beyond comprehension. If only he had had dark eyes
with a little touch of wickedness in them, he would have
been more acceptable to her. But Sir Percy's eyes were
uncompromisingly blue and did not improve with age;
they were getting watery, which only made their color
more objectionable. Still, she was used to having him
around. When she was impatient or sad, she could always tease him and that always made her feel younger.
His life span had proved longer than that of any dog,
cat or bird she had ever owned and, of course, now that
he was getting so old and a little dotty and very lonely,
she had developed a strong protective feeling toward
him. He was almost seventy now. She often wondered
what she would do if one day she was to get old herself.
She never quite felt that this could happen to her, but one
never knew. She still had a few good years left, but
after that, something was bound to happen. The only
thing, then, would be to retire among the flowers and
live entirely in one of her gardens, somewhere on the
Italian Riviera perhaps: flowers do not really care if

you are old or not, and they know how to make you feel younger.

Her smile became a little more tight and a little more ironic as she moved through the drawing room and accepted a cup of tea. The whole family was there and it all looked *awful*. She somehow couldn't quite believe that it was all hers, so to speak; that she had started it all, that without her, none of the twenty plain people in the room would have ever been born. It was quite incredible and a little embarrassing. Of course, she herself had only one son, so she couldn't *really* be blamed. She sipped her tea, observing them attentively and coldly, and she began almost to enjoy herself. You seldom saw a gathering of more serious, important, responsible people. What fun it would be to tell them, she thought, sipping her tea; how delightful it would be to watch their faces while their well-behaved world collapsed on their heads. She looked at their serious faces, at their discreet clothes, at the little refined cups of tea in their hands; she listened to the polite voices and she smiled a little, for it wouldn't do to laugh, as she wished to, it wouldn't do at all. She had been entirely successful in her revenge and she had kept her promise and now it did not matter any longer what she did or did not do. She could even take a lover, if she cared enough.

She wrapped the gay Indian shawl a little tighter around her shoulders. She loved cashmere shawls—or perhaps she simply loved to have something around her shoulders. It's extraordinary, she thought, how lonely your shoulders can become. In the end they don't even seem to belong to you and you have the feeling that they are strangers and that someone has forgotten them, left them behind. She stood there, wrapping herself in the Indian shawl, feeling its cozy, if a little artificial, warmth. The last forty years of her life had been nothing but a collection of wraps, hundreds of them—the best wools, the gentlest cashmeres—the warmest and the softest she could get. A woman shouldn't be left to look after her shoulders alone, she suddenly thought. But, of course, self-pity wouldn't do at all—it wasn't Parisian; and she was born Parisian, and had never really been anything but a woman of Paris. Percy was standing there, saying something, pleading with her.

"Such a wonderful life," he was saying. "So beautiful and noble in every respect. I really wish you would let me write your biography. It would be my greatest work—perhaps the only book that would survive me."

That was his main topic of conversation now: either he was asking her to let him write her biography or else he would plead with her to marry him, which was quite insulting, considering how old and unattractive he was. She looked him over severely, a little disapprovingly. It's truly extraordinary what becomes of human beings with the passing of years, she thought.

"Well, perhaps I will let you write my biography one day when I am old," she said lightly. "I'm only eighty today, so I'm afraid you will have to wait."

She lit a cigarette. She loved to smoke. She never inhaled but it was quite strange to be able to smoke in public—she couldn't quite get used to the idea that it was accepted nowadays. The children surrounded her with the usual compliments and presents and she had to pretend once again and express the usual appreciation. She had never really liked children, and the fact that some of the children were almost forty years old made it all even more ridiculous. Children should be kept in their place and if, admittedly, they could no longer be kept in the nursery, then they should stay in all the other childish places where they liked to gather and play—banks, parliaments, clubs, military headquarters—or some such things. Otherwise, they became rather a handful. One didn't know how to keep them quiet. They came to you with all sorts of ridiculous questions about your health—which was perfect, much better than theirs. Or else they bored you to death with their utterly ridiculous "problems": taxes, politics, money. People didn't seem to mind discussing money when the ladies were present nowadays; in the old days, this would have been considered as the mark of the beast. Or then they would talk politics, or even discuss *politicians*. In her days and in her circle, politicians were simply not mentioned. They were not accepted in the house—why, only a few statesmen could ever squeeze in. But now, they wouldn't even hesitate bringing some Americans to *dinner*. In her youth, when her first husband was alive, Americans simply did not exist—they hadn't yet been discovered. Yes, children were a nuisance. She didn't mind her little great-grandson so much, though. Such lovely dark eyes! She loved to take him on her knee, his little face turned to the light, and then she would talk to him patiently and play with him—so that he would allow her to look at his eyes, and to remember . . . Oh, well, it was no use getting sentimental again.

A chair had been prepared for her under the portrait of her first husband, and the photographer was summoned. No doubt, it would find its way into the *Tatler* or into the *Illustrated London News*—it always did. She had been considered a great beauty and she bore one of the greatest names in England. She knew exactly how to settle down in a chair, one hand on her cane, looking majestic and kindly, the perfect great-grandmother, surrounded by her children, under her portrait by Boldini, so that people would look at the picture in their clubs and feel reassured that the link with the past glories of England was still intact and that it was all not so long ago, and not quite gone. She took a look at the photographer and disliked him immediately. He was a swaying young man, mostly curves, and so respectful that he was almost rude. He really made one feel middle-aged. No manners. She sat there in the dignified pose that was expected from her, trying to look the kindly and distinguished, great old lady they wanted her to be, the famous, the splendid Lady L. But, of course, the smile would betray her, as always. That famous smile that Sargent, Jacques Émile Blanche and Boldini had all tried to recapture in their portraits. She had never liked any of the paintings that had been made of her: they all managed somehow to give her a certain airy touch of Victorian sweetness. She knew there was a certain cruelty in her smile, but the artists never permitted themselves to show it; they were too well paid and too respectful.

She had always been a little hard and a moment once came in her life when she had, she just *had* to be a little cruel. She well remembered a certain French saying: *"Celui qui aime bien, punit bien."* After all, she was born a *femme du peuple,* and for her, cruelty and violence always went together with love. She had never been in love with a gentleman, but what she knew of gentlemen made her doubtful that they could be either violent or cruel in love. They were either considerate or simply mediocre. She had known some English cads, true, but they were usually drinking or gambling cads, not loving cads.

The picture was taken, followed by the usual murmur of amiable small talk, and she had another hot cup of tea —there was nothing else, really, that one could do with the English. She talked with her granddaughters, whom, thank God, she didn't expect to see again till Christmas. None of the girls, now in their late thirties, were pretty —which was proper—and none of them knew how to dress, which was inexcusable. She longed to go away for her afternoon walk to the pavilion, but after all, it *was* her family and there were such things as manners. She exchanged a few remarks with Anthony, who was the most handsome of her grandsons and a churchman— *such* a waste! Yes, it all turned out all right, exactly as she had intended it.

As she watched them standing there with their cups

of tea, with their small talk, their discreet clothes and terrible hats, her smile became a little mischievous and she had to make an effort not to laugh. She simply longed to tell them—to tell them everything. It would be such fun. Just to see the horror, the shame and the incredulity on their faces. But, of course, it wouldn't do—it wouldn't do at all. She was not going to shatter their comfortable complacency. Why should she? She didn't care enough. Why shouldn't they be stuffy and conventional and successful in the pursuit of money and office? That's exactly how she had intended it to be.

It was then that she suddenly heard Jimmy talking and the words "summer pavilion" reached her ear, and then she heard him saying, "They are going to build a road through here, so it has to go."

She began to listen attentively. They had been trying to convince her to sell the pavilion for a long time now, and also part of the park and of the woods—taxes, apparently, were a big problem nowadays. She had always refused to pay the slightest attention to this silly talk, dismissing the whole subject with a shrug. But now, to her horror, she heard Jimmy saying that the government was going to expropriate the land to build a new road, and that the pavilion had to come down. There would be compensation, naturally, he concluded reassuringly. What sort of compensation? she suddenly thought bitterly. There were certain things lost that nothing in the world could ever replace.

"Stuff and nonsense," she said. "I am not going to give up the pavilion."

"But, my dear, there is nothing we can do about it," Jimmy said. "It's the law."

Well, the law had got to be changed and that was all there was to it. After all, they still knew the right people and they could take care of that little problem without disturbing her. As she had told them a hundred times before, the pavilion had a great sentimental value for her—she had some of her most favorite personal objects there. She liked to go there and sit there alone, just dreaming, remembering, thinking of her past. But for the first time since she had heard the subject discussed, the family didn't let the matter drop. They were nice to her, considerate, but very firm. The land and the pavilion had to go. There was simply nothing they could do about it. There would be a public outcry against them if the family so much as mentioned that it opposed the new road, which was supposed to bring prosperity and trade to the county. And, anyway, the decision was completely out of their hands. The work on the road wouldn't begin for another two or three months, but there was no

17

force on earth now that could save the summer pavilion. It just had to go. She suddenly felt frightened and almost in panic. The cup was shaking in her hand and she had to put it down.

"There must be a way," she said, "there always is . . ." Couldn't they simply go and talk to the Prime Minister? The old man knew her well—couldn't they just explain to him . . .

She broke down. She remembered suddenly that times had changed, that these were no longer the days when she had powerful friends, when such little problems could be dealt with at one of her weekend house parties and when she would have been obeyed instantly. She had outlived her world. She felt suddenly utterly lost and lonely and old—but that, too, she knew, was no longer respected, that, too, no longer carried any weight. . . . If the pavilion had to go, well, then she would soon have to go herself, for she was not willing to live alone. She needed company. And she was not going to plead with them or bother to explain. They would not understand—they were so conventional, so stuffy, and they didn't know about love. She would have to think it over —perhaps there was still some way out. Lady L. pulled the shawl tightly around her shoulders and suddenly, without a word, she left the room. They stood there rather bewildered and put out by her sudden disdainful and impatient exit and she could almost hear them saying, "She is getting a little eccentric. . . . Of course, she is *so* very old."

CHAPTER TWO

Silly had followed her, as he always did, unless expressly told not to. He was trotting behind her, still holding his cup of tea, and he was trying so desperately to be helpful and reassuring that she looked at him kindly and smiled at him through her tears. She knew that her smiles were big moments in his life and that he probably could remember all of them—there weren't too many. After all, he had been in love with her for almost fifty years and one had to be grateful. But he was such a bloody snob, Silly was! She wondered if she should tell him the truth: she wasn't sure at all that his heart, arteries and blood pressure could withstand it. It had taken him twenty-five years to get into White's and to get elected, and he had really turned himself into a statue of respectability; for if a well-born heel could easily become a member, a commoner had really to practice all the conventional virtues to make himself acceptable. She knew that she could tell him her secret only at the risk of seeing him drop dead from sheer shock and horror; on the other hand, she had to have some help. Something had to be done quickly. She could not allow the workers to tear the pavilion down and let all her precious objects be dispersed. Besides, there was one thing about Silly: he would never betray her or abandon her.

"My dear . . ."

"For God's sake, Percy, put your cup down. Your hands shake and it sounds awful. I never realized that your hands shake so much."

Silly looked hurt. "Seeing you cry would make me shake even if I were twenty. It has nothing to do with age."

"Well, put your cup down and listen to me," Lady L.

said. "I'm in an awful mess." She looked at him disapprovingly. "Now your knees are shaking, too. Really,
Percy, after all those years among gentlemen, you should
have learned not to have any feelings."

"You cannot expect me to see you crying and unhappy
without showing some concern," the Poet Laureate protested. "I wish I knew what's the matter . . ."

"Well, I'm going to tell you," Lady L. said. "I'm in a
mess, Percy. It's something about the pavilion and I cannot even mention it to the children. They are quite
likely to call the police. Not that it matters, really. I
wouldn't mind the scandal: it's about time I had *some*
fun. But there are certain things, certain objects, in the
pavilion that you simply *must* help me to save. They
have for me a great sentimental value. Also, I'm in
love, and I just have to share it with somebody—it might
as well be you. After all, you have written volumes and
volumes of love sonnets, so it's time for you to learn
something about love."

Silly looked crushed. He followed her, his head low,
toying with the ribbon of his eyeglasses, mumbling something apologetic. They went through the Boucher and
Fragonard rooms, then down the stairs, and through the
Tiepolo rooms—Tiepolo was her favorite—toward the
southern entrance of the house. She knew, of course, that

clouds, they somehow looked closer to a Johann Strauss waltz than to Johann Sebastian Bach, and in the end, when everything had been said, the fact remained, she had never accepted beauty without a certain air of light-ness and happiness about it: art was not meant to save the world, but just to make it more agreeable. It seemed to her that an artist who tried to achieve too much, even if he succeeded, was rather a bore. Perhaps she was too feminine to fully appreciate majesty, immortality and grandeur. She preferred something more emotional or pleasing, something closer to herself, elegant, frivolous or amusing. She loved her Boucher, her Fragonard, her Hubert Roberts, and the tender *grisailles* and the Italian *trompe l'oeil* that made the heavy walls suddenly open on a scene of laughter and gaiety. Works of art should really be pets, she thought, and one should be able to fondle them and not to treat them with awe and respect. An artist who was devoting himself too clearly to achiev-ing an immortal masterpiece was rather like a thinker or an idealist who was trying to save the world—and she had no patience with idealists.

All the objects, bibelots, *turqueries*, cheap paintings, pieces of odd furniture—she loved *things*—were kept in the summer pavilion, and when asked how she, whose taste had become almost legendary among the art dealers of the world, could cherish such junk—all this romantic trash, postcards, embroidery, rugs, love scenes in the moonlight, narghiles, cushions, third-rate paintings of the Bosporus, and thousands of objects that made the summer pavilion look like a huge, rich slice of Turkish delight—she would always give a very simple answer: they had for her, she would say, a great sentimental value. But now they were trying to take the pavilion away from her, to raze it to the ground, to disperse all the treasures she loved so much, to deprive her of the refuge where, every day, she spent hours in the happy and nostalgic company of *things*.

They were walking down the steps of the southern entrance now, Silly trying to offer her his arm and she pretending not to see it and resenting something that would have been perhaps still a courtesy a few years ago, but was now becoming merely an irritating implication of age. She was determined not to give up the pavilion without a fight. She had always fought for the things she loved. But she needed help. Even if the pavilion had to go, there were certain precious objects that she couldn't trust to anyone, and, although Percy was rather shaky, he could be still made to carry a few things to safety. So he *had* to be told. There was no other way. A thin smile came back to her lips and a touch of

light made her dark eyes gayer. In a way, she was going
to enjoy telling him. He would be so frightened!

"You will have to brace yourself for a shock, Percy."

He trotted rather nervously and a little suspiciously
by her side. He knew quite well that she was unpredictable. It had always been for him a source of wonder that
such a great lady should sometimes say certain things,
use certain words and laugh in such a—well, how to
put it?—in such an almost common way—and he had
often tried to understand how, in the aristocratic circle
she had always lived, she had managed to learn certain
expressions, and even gestures, that no one would have
really expected from her. Of course, she had always
been a little eccentric—and she was born French, too,
which also explained things. To this day, she still had a
trace of French accent and when she spoke English it
was very charming, and her French blood explained perhaps a certain vivacity of gesture, manners and voice.

"What is it, my dear?"

"It's a terrible secret. I'm simply wondering if you
are physically able to take it. How's your blood pressure?"

"Well, I have just had a complete checkup, from Sir
Hartley . . ."

The Poet Laureate felt a little uneasy. He never knew

what she would suddenly thrust at him. It had always been like that and, as he had kept her company almost constantly, he had finally ended up with a permanently scared, nervous, anticipating expression on his face. He looked at her imploringly, toying with the ribbon of his eyeglass.

"Please, darling, try to show yourself understanding. I know that you are a gentleman, but after all you are a writer as well—"

"Diana, nothing that you can do or have done could possibly be objectionable. In fifty years, I've never seen you do anything that did not do honor or give credit to you, your late husband, your name and your family."

She shook her head, almost in despair now. What a pompous old ass he had become. Years ago, it wasn't so noticeable because he was so good-looking. She had always loved good-looking men and she forgave them a lot. She even sometimes managed not to notice how stupid they were. But when they were getting old and their good looks were gone and there was nothing left but their trembling chins and flabby noses and tired eyes— then their minds became important. When they were beginning to breathe heavily after a waltz, when they were eating more and more to compensate for all the things they could no longer do, when their faces and their eyes and their lips had lost their fire—then they should really begin to make efforts and try to *understand* women, which was the only way left for them to please them. But when you are eighty, you can no longer pick and choose, and Percy at least could be relied upon to do exactly as he was told. What a pity, though, that he was such a bad writer. Great and true loves are few upon this earth and no one should have the right to let them vanish without leaving a trace. If only he could describe, convey, immortalize—but he was too *comme il faut* and too well bred to be able to deal with a love story. There was too much fire in it, it burned too bright, it hurt too deep and it exploded too much in flames, in pain and in delight. She looked at him sideways. Even with this white mane and this noble forehead and with the blue eyes, by no stretch of imagination could he be seen as an immortal bard. But perhaps he could tell something of her story, and then forever there would be someone to sigh, closing the book, and say: "She had loved."

She stopped suddenly and put a handkerchief to her eyes.

"If only you were Spanish, or French, or Italian . . . or something like that," she said, through her tears. "Perhaps you would be able to tell . . . to write it. Please do your best, Percy. Please do your best. . . ."

30

He was looking at her guiltily, imploringly. He was such a nice old thing. She knew that if he could, he would have agreed to turn himself into a Frenchman or even into an Italian immediately—and God knows there was nothing he would have found more distasteful. He tried to say something, but she knew that already he couldn't find the words. She smiled and touched his arm gently, reassuringly.

Then she began to speak. It was only half a mile's walk to the pavilion, if one followed the path between the chestnut trees. But there was another way, a shorter way, through the wilderness of bushes and cherry trees, of lilac and azalea, a few hundred yards of private jungle which she had carefully preserved untouched and free to do as it pleased. No gardener was ever allowed to touch it and the weeds were welcome and the bushes were sometimes left to grow across the path and join hands. Of all the glorious gardens she had owned, this was the corner dearest to her heart. But it was quite hopeless to try to drag Percy through it, and so they took the easier way. The sun was warm and the shadows pleasant. The leaves were still green and only when the light touched them did they suddenly seem to reach a sudden and golden maturity. The well-designed flower beds, the tea roses that were so appropriately called

"The English Afternoon," growing at a polite distance from each other and barely giving their fragrance away, the marble statues of coy nymphs and cupids that seemed to belong more to nurseries than to alcoves, the peaceful line of the hills sloping toward the sea and the lawn that seemed to await some gentle cricketer—all this was so familiar to her that she was no longer bothered by it, or oppressed by its placidity. Only the two black swans gliding slowly on the dreamy pond gave her the usual sharp twinge of pleasure and brought to her lips a passing smile of tenderness.

CHAPTER THREE

Annette Boudin was born in the Rue de Lappe—a strange accident, for the Rue de Lappe in the eighteen seventies was not a neighborhood where children were born, although there was no denying that a lot of what it takes to bring a child into the world was taking place there. The first moral influence to which Annette had been submitted in her early life came from her father: a big, powerfully built printer's hand, sitting

and sadistic urges, for the last-ditch thrill seekers, there was nothing more irresistibly attractive than the dangerous darkness, the vulgarity and the coarseness of the lower depths. Those who longed for a few minutes of self-destruction were irresistibly drawn toward the shadows of the Rue de Lappe, where the apache, with a scarf around his neck, and sometimes a flower in his teeth, would lean, immobile, against the lamppost, while for those who preferred other wares, the girls in high black boots were waiting against the wall.

Lady L. had always shrugged ironically at all the nineteenth-century melodramas in which the old *dépravé* and roué brings havoc and destruction and death through his longing for the innocent and the fresh. She knew that for the true *débauché*, the silk-hatted dreamers of the deep, who, after dinner, left their respectable wives or their aristocratic clubs for the appeal of the abyss, the company of the totally corrupt, of the completely low and sunken, was much more powerful and inspiring than that of virginal bloom. The top-hatted dandy was a familiar sight and the best provider of the Rue de Lappe. Vice had never been merely a pleasure; it had to be a drama, a total collapse, even if for a few seconds, a suicide, a cheap form of murder unpunishable by law, a liberation from all restraints, and for the brief moment of Apocalypse that could be purchased under the gaslight of the street, some of the best names of Paris didn't hesitate to risk their health and even their life.

The daily spectacle of the Rue de Lappe had been familiar to Annette from her cradle, and she had very early become immune and indifferent to it. She was told to help her mother wash the laundry almost as soon as she began to speak, and in the process she acquired a violent dislike for physical labor. Her father took some trouble over her education. She was only eight when she was taught spelling in the *Principles of Anarchy*, and at the age when other children were learning by heart the fables of La Fontaine, she was made to memorize the most juicy appeals to social revolt and then recite them to her proud parent, who would nod approvingly, sucking a smelly cigar. He would sit for hours on her bed, talking about the sacred rights of man and total freedom, while her mother toiled in the courtyard from five in the morning often until midnight. Sometimes Monsieur Boudin would bring in a few friends for a long discussion about the necessity of issuing a warning to society by throwing a bomb into the Parliament. She would have understood their noble aspirations better if they had come down into the yard and given her mother a hand. At one time, they became particularly aggressive about a German called Karl Marx, whose ideas apparently consisted of doing away with private property by giving it to the State. But for them, the State, or any other form of organized society, was the root of all evil, and they went on shaking their fists and banging the table and explaining to each other that Marx had to be assassinated, even before the Pope, if true freedom was to survive.

It was probably by listening to her father talk while her mother worked herself to death—she died of consumption when Annette was only thirteen—that she had acquired a strongly practical turn of mind and a violent dislike for big words and those noble idealistic feelings to which her father always referred in his drunken, emotional, tenor voice as the "noblest aspirations of the human soul." It seemed to her then that it was not so much the soul as the body that mattered: it suffered, toiled, sweated and died. And if it was true that the soul lived forever, then truly there was no reason to worry about it. If you had a strong, healthy and happy body, the soul would take care of itself. After her mother had died, her father took it for granted that she would keep the laundry going, and so she did, for a while, while her father would show his appreciation and gratitude for his daily bread and cheese by explaining to her how all their problems would be solved through the destruction of the family, the liberation of the individual from the State and the access to the natural freedom, to something, he would explain to her enthusiastically, his eyes misty, his voice throaty, something that would make them all as happy as the animals are when left to follow their natural ways. She listened to him while ironing her sheets and staring at him attentively, making up her mind. She knew well enough that there was an easier way of making a living and although she had no illusions about its hardships and dangers, she soon decided that there was for her no other way out: she somehow didn't quite believe that her father and his friends would really make the world a better place.

She had hesitated quite a bit, but as if to help her make up her mind, her father took a hand. Monsieur Boudin would often come to Annette's room with a bottle of absinthe in his hand, pour some green liquid into his throat and, after a few heavy sighs, would begin to look at Annette with his soulful eyes, so full of aspirations and longings that they almost stood out of their sockets like the eyes of the cockroaches running about the kitchen floor. He would then make another long speech against the family as an institution and explain how it was essential to liberate children and parents from that bourgeois relationship. Annette, half asleep in

her bed, didn't listen. She was too tired and too desperate. But then the attacks against the family institution
became more precise, more explicit. Monsieur Boudin
would come closer to his daughter and make it quite
clear what he meant when he said that daughters and
fathers should be liberated from their bourgeois relationship and made truly free . . . and it soon became
quite clear how he intended to put into practice his
anarchist theories about family life. Annette would then
grab a rolling pin and knock him on the head, and
Monsieur Boudin would then retire with his absinthe,
grumbling and moaning and cursing his daughter for
having become herself a slave of the bourgeois morality
and, making a last stand at the door, the bottle in one
hand, the other on his heart, he would call on her to
rise from bondage and to break free from conventional
morality, so that human beings could become beautiful and happy, as nature wanted them to be.

Annette soon realized that, even if she wanted to, she
could not keep the laundry going, simply because she
didn't have the strength and the determination, or rather
the resignation, of her mother. And, of course, the
apaches of the Rue de Lappe never stopped making
offers to her, always willing to help. Why was she refusing so stubbornly to *faire la vie?* It's easy money

and for a girl like you, they said, with no one to look after you, there was no other way and there never would be any other way. Strangely enough, she was herself a little surprised by the resistance she put up against their offers. It was not that she was ashamed or had any scruples—she had nothing of the sort. Her eyes were hard and life had stared into them much too brutally to leave her any such illusions. It was much simpler than that: she had a strong, an almost sentimental attachment to cleanliness, perhaps because she had been brought up in a laundry.

She was fifteen then and so she considered the situation coldly and practically, with the strong French common sense that was never to desert her completely, even in her deepest moments of passion, devotion, longing and love. She had tried to find work in other quarters of Paris—any decent work would do, she didn't mind. She had looked for work in millinery shops, in cafés, restaurants, in pastry shops and street fairs and she had immediately found out that there too she would have to sleep with a man, either to get work, or to keep it. She was much too pretty to be left alone. She soon decided that it was better to start her life on the *trottoir* than to end it there, and if she began young and pretty enough, perhaps she could escape it quicker—there was nothing more horrible to her than the sight of the middle-aged prostitutes waiting in the darkest corners of the street, where the light couldn't quite reach them. Once she had made her decision, she went about it with her typical, no-nonsense, straightforward way: her first customer was more surprised than pleased. She took the visitors to her miserable lodgings, while her father sat in the next room, talking louder and louder about the immortal aspirations of the human soul and pretending with a great sense of personal dignity not to notice on what source of income he was fed, clothed, and occasionally supplied with a bottle of absinthe. But after he had renewed in his circuitous but unmistakable way his attacks against certain bourgeois *préjugés* of family life, she threw him out of the house. It was then that Monsieur Boudin, immediately forgetting his eloquent attacks against the family as an institution, called upon Heaven itself to witness how ungrateful his daughter was and how cruelly she treated her only parent.

A few months later, Monsieur Boudin was found floating in the brown waters of the Seine with a knife in his back. It was then discovered, or rather it then became widely known, that he had been working for the police as an *agent provocateur*, denouncing his anarchist friends to the authorities. He had been personally

responsible for the arrest of the famous anarchist Je-
rome, who had held up the Bank de Paris on the Boule-
vard des Italiens. When Annette was called to the Poste
de Police and asked to identify the body, she glanced
at her parent's face, which still wore a noble expression
of indignation, and then turned to the two gendarmes
who were the same two mustachioed fellows who had so
often come to fetch her father and whom she used to
call *Liberté* and *Egalité*. She took out of her purse three
coins of five francs each, gave them two and threw the
third on the table.

"Give it to *Fraternité*," she said, and walked out.

Lady L. stopped by the pond, and, taking out of her
pocket a few pieces of bread she always carried with her
for the birds—there were also nuts for the squirrels—
she leaned over the water and offered them to the two
black swans who began to glide toward her slowly and
majestically. Sir Percy Rodiner waited, his hands
crossed behind his back. He looked a little reproachful.
He even went so far as to show a slight trace of disapproval on his face.

"My dear Diana," he said. "I simply cannot see what
those unsavory, to say the least, characters and incidents
have to do with the summer pavilion, and why you deem

it necessary to tell me these horrors. How on earth you can know of such things is beyond my comprehension."

Lady L. did not seem to listen. She was feeding the swans. She had always kept black swans in all her gardens and she never tired of looking at them. Life was full of beauty and it was sometimes difficult to say what one admired most, but perhaps a black swan would be her first choice.

"She was such a lovely girl, Annette was," she said with a sigh, throwing the last piece of bread into the water. "She knew it, too. Whenever she looked at herself in the mirror, she instinctively felt that one day the world would be at her feet. In those times, of course, there still was such a thing as having the world at your feet. . . . Oh well, we'll all have to age one day. Yes, she was very beautiful. I can say it without feeling conceited or vain because it was all so long ago. . . . Sixty-five years ago, to be precise. It was *almost* as if she were a different person, a stranger, not me at all. . . ."

The Poet Laureate seemed suddenly to have been turned into a statue. There were other statues around the pond, among the flower beds: cupids and goddesses, Apollos and Pans playing their lutes, and Percy suddenly seemed to have become part of the family. His

44

mouth gaped, his face turned ghastly white and the eyes took on a hurt expression under the noble brows. Lady L. looked him over with a certain satisfaction. After all, Percy's dream had always been to have a statue of himself, made by some member of the Royal Academy, standing in one of the more fashionable squares with a laurel wreath on its head. Well, this was almost it. Perhaps the expression of his face was not exactly the one with which he hoped to face posterity, but you couldn't have *everything*.

"For God's sake, Silly, don't have a stroke. It would be *too* difficult," she said. "You look exactly like Bon Bon, my white Pekingese, when the poor little thing had his heart attack. Really, Silly, it was all a very long time ago. It has all been made clean now. Time washes everything, you know. Don't throw a fit."

For the first time in a long and distinguished career of discretion and self-effacement, Sir Percy let go.

"Damn it, Diana, do you mean to say that you and that awful girl are the same . . . But it's preposterous! I refuse to believe it. You have always loved to shock people, but this is really going too far. And on your birthday, too. You bear one of the most famous names in England, your life is an open book, full of grace and beauty, and here, suddenly, you try to suggest. . . . Of course, I know all this is pure invention, but even so it's quite unpalatable. I refuse to listen."

Lady L. took him gently under the arm.

"Come on, Percy, I always keep brandy in the pavilion. You need a drink. Why should I bother to invent things? My life has been far more exciting and wonderful than any fairy tale. Of course, I am Annette—or was—and believe me, a very lovely thing I was, too. And anyway, it all happened *abroad*, so it's quite all right."

But Sir Percy refused to budge.

"Damn it, damn it, damn it!" he repeated. "You have treated me badly long enough. I am not going to stand it a moment longer. You have no business trying to make me believe this sort of thing about yourself, Diana. I feel . . . I feel betrayed. After all, I have my pride. For fifty-odd years I have been your most devoted admirer and I shall not accept, even from you, that the everything I looked up to with such respect and love has been suddenly destroyed. I have loved you all my life and it's my right to defend the object of my love and I refuse you the right to try to smash it to pieces."

Lady L. almost hit him with her cane.

"Now then, Silly, don't be such a stuffy fool. Nobody will know of this at Boodle's or White's—or whatever club you belong to. You've just got to listen to me. I am telling you the story because I need your help and if, by the time I have finished, you still don't believe it, I'll show you the proof. It's all there, in the pavilion. Oh, dear, why is it that men are such prudes nowadays? I've known some real men in my time and you couldn't knock them down with a feather. After all, you have been pestering me for years for permission to write my biography and now, when I begin to tell you *something* of my life, you get in such a state— It's time for you to learn about women, Percy. You know, I sometimes suspect you are still a virgin."

The Poet Laureate slowly put the monocle into his right eye.

"Diana, I must ask you . . ."

"All right, all right, let's walk. Let's imagine I'm telling you a story. You will believe me or not, as you please. But you will still have to help me. Even if it is all a little shocking for a person of your age."

One evening as she was waiting for customers in the street, Annette saw coming toward her a young apache by the name of René la Valse, a little thin, blond man, who was at the time acting as a liaison between the underworld of the Rue de Lappe and the police. During

several years, a sort of truce, if not quite a gentlemen's
agreement, was established between the gendarmes and
the underworld kings, by which both sides acknowledged
their mutual existence and franchise, the police depart-
ment keeping its nose out of the street with the understanding that none of the *fils de famille* aristocrats,
politicians, rich bourgeois from the *beaux quartiers*,
while on their slumming expeditions, would be found
in the gutter with their throats cut. Annette could always
recognize René la Valse in the dark by his bronchial
breathing. He suffered from an advanced case of tuberculosis, but in spite of this, he was one of the best
dancers of *java* in the street. He would dance for hours,
and then come out and sit on the *trottoir*, breathing
with difficulty, and saying, shaking his head sadly,
"The doctor says I shouldn't dance at all. It's bad for
my lungs."

But then as the music would burst out again, he
would kick his heels and rush onto the floor with a
rose behind his ear, the favorite of all the girls; they
provided for his various needs and then he would show
off for hours again at the *bal musette*, until a coughing
fit would stop him in the middle of a *pas*. Now, René
la Valse came running toward her, panting with excitement or tuberculosis, she didn't know which.

"Quick, Annette— Monsieur Lecoeur wants to see you."

She stood still a moment, pressing her heart, for she knew instantly that fate was taking a hand, as she had always believed it would. She had always known somehow that the best things of life would be hers.

Alphonse Lecoeur was then the most famous pimp in Paris—*souteneur* was the right word, for he no longer stood in the streets, counting the customers, but owned a *hotel particulier* and carriages and horses, gambled and lost heavily at the best gambling places in Paris, managed several boxers successfully for the sake of sport, thus gaining an introduction to some of the English lords and young bloods of French society who didn't mind the company of a *canaille* as long as he had style and money. He was considered untouchable by the police because he was in a position to blackmail not only the Chief of Police himself, but some of the great names of the Republic, and was said to have disposed, in his rise from the gutter, of at least half a dozen rivals. His appearance had a lot to do with his success in the so-called sporting society of the Paris of that day. He was powerfully built, with shoulders that were almost as large as those of the famous Zouave of the *pont d'Alma,* an enormous chunk of flesh, both in face and in body. His

49

cheeks were brick-colored, his thick eyebrows were only matched by the heavy mustache that cut the face in two, like a bar of blackness, and he had fixed, strangely gleaming eyes, where the irises and the pupils were all merged in the same gleaming darkness. Dressed with eccentric pretentiousness, in a brown-and-black checked suit, a red waistcoat, with a golden chain, his fingers heavy with ruby and diamond rings, he stood there under the lamppost, with a brown derby hat slightly tipped over one ear, smoking one of those famous cigars that never left his lips.

By his side stood his inseparable companion, less than half his size, an Irish jockey, known, for some mysterious reason, by the name of Sapper, changed by the Parisian underworld into a more familiar, if much longer, *Saperlipopette*. He was dressed in sporting clothes, wearing a cap over his sad, elongated and narrow face, with a strange expression of permanent protest and reproach spread over his features. His head was permanently twisted and tilted to one side and he couldn't move his neck without moving his whole body. He had once been the most famous jockey in England, but had broken his neck in Paris riding for his English master in the Grand Prix du Bois. He had drifted aimlessly through Paris, soon forgotten by the noble lord whose horses he had ridden to so many victories. He then was taken up by Alphonse Lecoeur, perhaps because the latter's megalomania felt flattered by the diminutive size of the jockey at his side, which made his own stature loom even larger. They had soon become inseparable and Sapper bestowed upon Alphonse Lecoeur his complete devotion and gratitude. Such were the two men who were now looking Annette over, and Lecoeur puffed his cigar without a word, while René la Valse cringed nervously in the shadows, looking at the great man.

It was only much later that Annette was told how the attention of Alphonse Lecoeur had been drawn by his scouts to the new girl in the Rue de Lappe, a girl whose young loveliness and natural grace caught their experienced eye very shortly after Annette had started on her new profession. It was not simply that she was very beautiful. There were plenty of lovely girls in Paris and, in fact, that was what rendered the choice so difficult to make. For the purpose Alphonse Lecoeur had in mind, beauty was not enough. A quick mind, the ability to learn and to remember, a natural poise and grace, ambition and a lot of courage were essential. For the career of Alphonse Lecoeur had taken, at that time, a strange and unexpected turn. At the height of his power, feared by the underworld and police alike, able to dictate his terms

both to the law and to its enemies, he had suddenly discovered that this was no longer enough. Ten years of
success in crime made him suddenly feel that his was
not an ordinary mind, that he was far above the crowd,
that in a way, he was born to lead, to do and to undo—
but he simply didn't know how to use the power he had
in hand. He was not an intelligent man and he had never
read a book, but he began to search for some sort of
intellectual justification, for something that would give a
meaning to his life. He suddenly began to look for an
intellectual excuse for his career of crime. He began to
think of himself as a great man with a purpose, and
although he couldn't quite see what this purpose was, in
the eighties there were men around who were ready to
explain it all to him willingly, and to tell him that if he
had become an outlaw, it was because deep in his heart
he was an enemy of all organized society, that he was,
in fact, an anarchist.

Among those men was the young anarchist Armand
Denis.

Armand Denis was the only son of a respectable, con-
servative family from the city of Rennes. In his early
years he had been a devout and deeply mystical youth,
with a natural gift for oratory that had made him the
pride of his Jesuit school, and destined to become one

day a priest himself. He was sent to a seminary in Paris and it was there, in the big city, that his faith left him in the most sudden and dramatic way. He was to write later in his *Age of Revolt* that it was while walking through the poor quarters of Paris, among the drunks, the prostitutes and the destitute, that such a violent hatred for injustice, for pain and poverty and helplessness and ugliness overtook him that his faith suddenly gave place to a determination not to wait for heaven to put things right. He turned eagerly toward the great fighters against injustice, toward Proudhon, toward Reclus and toward Karl Marx, but they had all left him angry and unsatisfied. The craving for absolute justice which burned in his heart and mind and to which he was now refusing to give the name of God as an answer was such that they all seemed too moderate, too patient. For Karl Marx his dislike had been instant and violent: the German still thought in terms of organized society, and this, in his eagerness for absolute freedom, which once, as a religious youth, he had wanted for the soul in heaven, but which he now claimed for body and mind as well, was unacceptable and wrong. It seems that it was in his own thoughts more than in the books of the more conventional apostles of anarchy that Armand Denis had found the inspiration for his theories and for his future tragic deeds.

He broke with the church and the seminary in a most shocking and brutal manner. One morning at the Cathedral of Notre Dame, when the crowd of the faithful was waiting for the priest to begin the Mass, a young, strangely beautiful youth, with a fanatical white face and burning, dark eyes, mounted to the pulpit. It was as if a dark angel had suddenly appeared above the crowd. He was still wearing the black seminarist's clothes that accented his pallor and for one second there was an even deeper silence in the cathedral, for the appearance of the young man and his extraordinary good looks filled them all with expectation and awe. And then, suddenly, the exquisite white hands lifted something into the air for all to see—it was a dead rat which he held by the tail.

"Look, God is dead!" he exclaimed, in a voice that seemed to fill the cathedral with hatred. "God is dead! It is up to you free men of good will to take your fate into your own hands."

The blasphemer was seized immediately and thrown first into jail, and then, on the suggestion of his family that he had suddenly become insane, he was locked up for several months in the lunatic asylum of Sainte Anne, which saved from extreme embarrassment not only his family but the Fathers who had educated him and who nursed such high hopes for his future. The terrible months in the asylum inflamed him with a new bitterness and with an even stronger determination to regenerate the world. He was determined to save mankind from ugliness—and there was no greater ugliness than injustice, poverty, police, authority, and money. His anarchist creed was born and was never to leave him. It was the intention of his family to keep him in the lunatic asylum until things were forgotten, and until he himself began to show some regret for what he had done. He had no great difficulty in escaping from Sainte Anne, but it was only to find himself in the streets without money or friends, hungry, lonely, tortured by his impatience to change the world. Passers-by stared in wonder at the white-faced youth in shoddy black clothes, bareheaded, staring with his inspired eyes toward some distant horizon of beauty and justice and universal love. Quite naturally, he soon found his way toward the poorest and more disreputable quarters of Paris, where it was easier to hide and make friends. He began mixing with criminals, whom he saw as victims and enemies of society and thus his natural allies. They fed him, clothed him, patted him on the back and listened with amusement to his speeches, while he explained to them that deep in their hearts they were frustrated idealists who had turned toward crime because it was the only way to fight and show their scorn of the hated bourgeois. They never took him quite seriously, although it was pleasant to hear that every pickpocket had a social purpose deep in his heart, that every apache was unknowingly an idealistic rebel and every prostitute a noble victim of the rich.

But the one man who lent him an attentive ear and sometimes listened for hours, fascinated by his inflamed speeches, was Alphonse Lecoeur. What the young anarchist was saying gave him exactly the justification and the purpose he was looking for. Yes, yes, it was all true; he was an enemy of society, he was a rebel, a *révolté*, and if he had become a pimp, a murderer, a blackmailer, and a king of the underworld, it was merely because he was fighting against the established order with all the means at his disposal. Yes, crime was a form of terrorism, exploiting the rich was like throwing a bomb, and a refusal to live by the accepted standards of society was a sign of a noble revolt. Alphonse Lecoeur would stroll from tavern to tavern looking for the young anarchist, and then he would listen to him, half hidden by the crowd, pretending to be merely amused, standing there with his big cigar. The jockey stood by his side, with his twisted, tilted, frozen neck and his sad, elongated face. Armand Denis had soon noticed that he had made a powerful convert, but he took great care not to show it. He was determined not to approach him until he was ready—ready not only to listen, but to follow, not only to help, but to obey.

Armand was then only twenty-six years old and there was no woman who looked at him who didn't feel like a mother or a mistress. There was something in his face that was more than beauty: a burning inspiration, a poetry that was made of lips and eyes and brow, something both violent and tender, something that one wanted to protect and to love. He had already published his famous *Age of Revolt*, and although there was a call to murder on every page, one was more struck by its poetry and the beauty of its style than by his black designs. He had been thrown in jail several times for his incendiary speeches in public places and for the distribution of subversive literature.

The French anarchists of that time, all under the influence of Proudhon, Bakunin and Reclus, had broken with him, for it appeared to them that in his eagerness for individual action he ran the risk of compromising the chances of the movement as a whole. They had re-

lands, and hoping that somehow the echo of their words would inflame the world and achieve their aims.

For Armand, words, exciting as they were, were not enough. Perhaps because he was a dreamer he was determined to become a man of action. It is not known for certain that it was he himself who had shot and killed the famous Commissaire de Police, Monsieur Antoine, in 1880. But he had been credited with it and this made his position among his friends the criminals very precarious. The last thing the *milieu* wanted was a war with the police. The killing appeared as a breach of their gentlemen's agreement, and Armand Denis learned that he was to be denounced as a price for continuing good relations between the police and the underworld. It was then that the young man decided to turn for help to Alphonse Lecoeur, and, although he judged him for what he was, stupid and vain, he also knew of his *folie de grandeur*, of his desire to give a meaning to his career of crime and to go down in history as a man with a purpose, the avenging Robin Hood of the streets of Paris.

In the middle of the night, Armand went to see Lecoeur in the back of a gambling house, where the latter used to spend the early hours of the morning. The place was run by an orange-haired, crooked-nosed, white-powdered Baronne de Chamisse, who merely acted as a screen for Lecoeur. The Baronne, the petrified waves of her wig engulfing her head, a black velvet ribbon around her neck and tortoise-shell lorgnette in her hand, conducted Armand into an empty gambling room, where he was soon joined by Lecoeur, still fondling some gold napoleons which he had won. Then Armand Denis began to talk. He knew his man and he knew how to talk.

"It's time for you to show your real stature. There are still people who see you merely as a panderer, as a common bandit and racketeer. They don't even suspect that you have chosen crime because it is the only way left for you to fight a society you despise. Each of your deeds is a protest and a challenge. Your name could soon be loved and praised by millions of enslaved peoples everywhere, a modern Robin Hood, enemy of the bourgeois and a savior of the poor. For a man of your stature, it's not enough to be *feared*; you must be *loved* and you must be *followed*. You have already done a lot to break the power of the police, but your motives and your purpose remain obscure and to many you still appear as a mere criminal. . . ."

Alphonse Lecoeur, standing by the green table, was still fondling his gold napoleons. His heavy face was flushed with pride and he was seeing himself, at last, in Armand's words, as a man of meaning, of ideal and of destiny. Had he lived in later days, he would probably have become a Fascist, like another criminal, Horst Wessel, who had helped Hitler in his rise to power, or he would have looked toward a man like Benito Mussolini, who had, in his youth, been so close to the anarchists himself. For it was the future dictator of Italy who had translated Kropotkin's *Paroles d'un Révolté*, describing the book of the anarchist prince as written "with a great love for oppressed humanity and with infinite kindness." But in those days the *libertaire* or anarchist movement seemed the only way for a man like Lecoeur to justify his past and give a social meaning to his crimes. That night, Armand Denis had made himself a lifelong ally and a strangely devoted and faithful friend. Perhaps there was more than simple ambition in Lecoeur's heart and, in a groping, confused way, he was truly trying to give a meaning to his destructive existence. Whatever the reason, the fact was that he threw himself entirely behind Denis, that he sought his company whenever he could and actually became somber and irritable, even unapproachable, when Armand Denis was away, as if he could find his reason for existence only in the young anarchist's words and presence.

62

At the gathering of the "cell" in some attic of Paris, the broad-shouldered, towering figure of Alphonse Lecoeur, in his dandy's clothes, would appear with the jockey at his side and watch him silently while Armand described their next step, or while a little gray-haired, innocent-looking professor of chemistry from the Lycée Louis le Grand would explain to them in a thin, eunuch's voice how to make bombs in the kitchen, or how to blow up a whole building by tampering with the gas reservoir.

The members of the cell were a strange lot: a street-organ player, who always brought his monkey along, a teacher of literature at a famous institution for *jeunes filles,* one of the best schools in Paris, a young worker, Villain, who some years later was to throw a bomb into the Chamber of Deputies, and Monsieur Poupat, a state calligrapher, whose beautiful handwriting was used by the government for the most important documents, diplomatic passports, special permits and official degrees. Alphonse Lecoeur would listen to them, nodding approvingly, and from time to time, trying to make his mark, he would launch into some effort of oratory on his own. He would point at the stiff-necked jockey, his head permanently twisted to one side, which always gave him the look of someone who watches the world critically, and he would exclaim hoarsely:

63

"Look at him, comrades! His neck was broken in the service of some English milord and when he could ride no more, they left him like a dog. So now there is only one desire in his heart and it is to plant a bomb at the Paris racetrack and to blow up a few of the noble lords."

In April 1881 a bomb was thrown on the racetrack of the Bois, where three horse-owners and one English trainer fell wounded under a shower of gray top hats. No one suspected the sad-faced jockey as he stepped forward from a panic-stricken crowd, picked up a top hat as a trophy and left the turf. No one had yet thought of Alphonse Lecoeur and his tiny associate as anything but criminals with powerful protection, and for a time at least the two remained above suspicion. Lecoeur appeared to be so much a part of the established order on which he preyed, he had such an obvious stake in it, that it was difficult to credit him with a subversive purpose. Had he contented himself with helping Armand secretly, he would have remained safe. But his inflated ego caused him more and more to move into the foreground and he was now openly speaking of himself as of an inspired leader of revolt and of his crimes as part of a plan to destroy society. His allies in high places were becoming more and more embarrassed, and the police could no longer ignore him.

As long as he had remained a mere criminal he could be tolerated as part of the existing order, but as soon as subversive political dogma had begun to find its way into his words and to loom behind his actions, he was becoming an enemy. His informers in the police had repeatedly warned him of danger, but he was too sure of himself and he dismissed their warnings with a shrug of his powerful shoulders. Cautiously, the police began to prepare for Lecoeur's arrest. It was a difficult move: he knew too much about too many. Then one of his most powerful victims, whom he had supplied with drugs, died of an overdose of opium. He knew that the game was up. But even then he could still be seen walking with Sapper on the boulevards or driving in a yellow carriage in the Bois. It was Armand Denis who finally convinced him to leave the country.

Switzerland, at that time, had become the refuge and gathering place of the anarchists from all corners of Europe. There they were allowed to meet freely and to publish their newspapers; the first Anarchist International had been tentatively set there in 1881. Armand knew himself unpopular with its leaders and he was determined to act strictly on his own, recruiting workers and agents who would accept both his program and his views. But to be independent and to carry out his ambitious plans he needed vast sums of money. Here again, Switzerland was the ideal place to get it. It was the playground of the rich; it was there that the wealthiest people of Europe drifted in their leisure. Also, all the great names of the *Almanach de Gotha* and *Burke's Peerage* were meeting there, among the mountain peaks and around the limpid—and languid—lakes. His plan was very simple. He intended to organize a series of well-planned burglaries and then use the money to stage a few spectacular coups against the crowned heads of Europe who gathered cozily in fashionable resorts and picturesque spas. He knew that it wouldn't be easy; he needed a lot of information from somebody who would know the right people and serve as an accomplice on the inside. Armand Denis had been thinking it all over with his characteristic thoroughness, laying his careful plans long ahead. He had decided that his best card would be a beautiful young woman, with the manners of a lady and a good mind that could understand his teachings, but who, once indoctrinated, would work secretly for him with the ardor of a disciple. It was for this purpose that Annette was summoned before Lecoeur and taken, without a word of explanation, to a *maison* in the Rue de Furcy and there introduced to Armand Denis.

Sir Percy Rodiner had to sit down. It was fortunate that one of the stone benches was only a few paces away—and even so, he barely managed to make it. His face expressed such an utter bewilderment and he looked so ghastly that Lady L. felt almost sorry for him. She hadn't expected him to take it all so hard. As she sat down by his side, once more putting her hand reassuringly on his arm, he gave her a quick, frightened look and moved away a little.

"Oh dear, oh dear," she said. "You *do* get in a state."

She tried to find something reassuring to say, something comforting.

"Come on, Percy dear," she said. "It's all right. There'll always be an England."

The Poet Laureate stiffened perceptibly.

"I must beg you, Diana, to keep England out of it," he said emphatically. He was staring ahead of him, his face a stricken mixture of sorrow and fright. His head trembled a little and there were tiny beads of sweat on his forehead. He took a handkerchief out of his pocket, unfolded it—Silly always had had the biggest handkerchiefs in the Western Hemisphere—and wiped his brow.

"I suppose it's only your damned sense of humor," he said in a shaky voice. "I don't believe there is a word of truth in it, not a word. Your background is perfectly known, and this is all pure invention. You were born Mademoiselle de Boisserignier, and one of your ancestors fought in the battle of Crécy . . ."

"We had great difficulty in forging those papers," Lady L. said. "It was particularly important to make the Crécy part look convincing. Monsieur Poupat, the state calligrapher, did a very good job of it, and then Armand himself had a go at it with chemicals. It was all rather fun."

Sir Percy opened his mouth, but no word came out. He took his handkerchief again and applied it to his forehead.

The late afternoon was warm and mellow. There was a sweet fragrance in the air: it came all the way from the lilac bushes around the pavilion. And there was also laughter, and voices coming from the lawn, where the children were starting a game of croquet.

The establishment in the Rue de Furcy was a shoddy place and closed to customers at that late hour of the night. There were only three girls there, wearing their high-buttoned boots, but in various degrees of undress: one of them in black lace drawers to her knees and a black corset, with her breasts bare, and two others fully dressed in green, orange and yellow organdy. Their faces white with powder, they were staring stupidly at the back of the man sitting by the piano. Annette didn't know it then, but she was witness to one of those strange exploits that made the name of Armand Denis so famous in those days. For the virtuoso sitting in his elegant evening dress at the piano was none other than the greatest pianist of his time, Anton Krajewski.

The next day's newspapers were full of indignant reports of the kidnaping. After the evening performance for the Parisian elite which paid a fortune to get tickets for the concert, the pianist, leaving the hall, was approached by Armand himself, in white tie, black top hat and silk-lined cape. Sticking a pistol concealed under his cape against Krajewski's back, Armand forced him into a carriage and brought him to one of the lowest brothels in Paris, ordering him to play for the prostitutes. When Annette entered the place, the maestro had already been playing for more than an hour. He was to say later that he had really had to give his best, because the young anarchist was a connoisseur of music and whenever Krajewski became a little too slack, he would reprimand him severely.

"Oh, no," he would say. "That won't do at all. I know, of course, that you are willing to do your best only before the very rich, before those who can afford to pay you. Now it is true these unfortunate ladies here are perhaps not the elite, but they are more in need of great music than any of your corrupt audiences."

As Annette came in, Armand, standing by the piano, was still holding the pistol in his hand. He smiled to her and then said quietly and almost sadly, "Come in, Mademoiselle, and listen to the concert. This gentleman here has spent his life playing for tyrants, for rulers, monarchs, princes and the very rich. So I brought him here to play, for once, for the exploited and the downtrodden, for the abandoned and the betrayed."

He turned his pistol toward the pianist.

"Play, maestro! Play! This is your first *clean* audience. This is the moment for you to do your best."

Years later, Anton Krajewski was to write in his memoirs that his indignation had vanished in the face of such deep conviction and obvious longing for some absolute, universal justice—that there was something deeply moving and sincere and pathetic in that voice that seemed to carry in its accent some desperate hope and pain. The dark young man standing there with the pistol in his hand and his incredibly handsome face and burning eyes was a tragic sight he was never to forget.

Krajewski was then in his later years, but he had

never put more of himself into his playing than he did that night. He played as a tribute to the impossible ideal of total justice that sometimes burned into a man's soul and reduced it, through its sheer immensity, to ashes.

Armand Denis was to repeat this strange feat several times in his career. Once, at the height of the Paris opera season, he had kidnaped the conductor Serafini and brought him to a flophouse by the Seine canal, where an assortment of vagabonds were busy scratching their fleas. There, before this pathetic flotsam of life, the maestro— white tie, baton in hand—was asked to conduct an imaginary orchestra and, for hours, was kept there, like a gesticulating puppet, before his nightmarish audience, which roared with laughter at the pantomime and wouldn't even allow him to stop long enough to wipe the sweat that poured from his scared face. As years went by, perhaps because his ideal was beginning to look farther and farther away, Armand Denis was to become more cruel, and he seemed sometimes to strike out of despair and not out of hope.

The three prostitutes didn't even listen, looking merely frightened. As for Annette, she was hardly conscious that there was music, for since the very moment she had entered the place, everything that was not the strangely lovely face before her suddenly seemed to have disappeared. At last Armand allowed the concert to end, and leaving the pianist to the care of Alphonse Lecoeur and the jockey, he took Annette upstairs. He had barely glanced at her. They came up the spiral narrow staircase into the ugly room and he stopped by the window and looked into the night and went on talking, as if she were not there at all and as if only the stars were listening.

"Art is premature," he was saying. "Beauty for the few is bad enough. But there is worse—even if all the people were given access to it, in our time of ugliness, art would merely be used as an opiate to make the slaves forget their slavery. I hate and despise all the great composers, painters and poets, who go on performing like circus dogs while nine tenths of the world are kept in poverty and squalor. Art is reactionary in its essence because, like alcohol, it merely tends to make people forget their unhappiness. The greatest artists today serve as a camouflage of ugliness. The painters, the poets and musicians of today help the police: they are here to keep order."

He was to repeat this speech many times during their time together, and Lady L. remembered every word of it. Only years later when all had been lost did she come to think of Armand as a great poet who had deliberately silenced himself and had refused to sing because the world was too ugly and had to be changed first. But there, in the little room, when he seemed to be talking to the night and the invisible sky as if asking for some impossible help, she wasn't listening. She was merely aware of the beating of her heart and her eyes were opened wide and she smiled in wonder. She was never to forget the first feeling of excitement and warmth that had overtaken her so suddenly as she stood there, her hand pressed against her breast, confronted by the first lovely sight that her young eyes had seen.

Lady L. was crying. She took a lace handkerchief from her pocket and raised it to her eyes.

"Oh, well," she said, "I mustn't, really."

Sir Percy sat stonily by her side. His face wore a solemn expression, both injured and determined, which he usually reserved only for Britain's darkest hours: when the first German bombs had come down on London, when the battleship *Prince of Wales* was sunk, when the Labour Party came into power and when Dicky Mountbatten, the last Viceroy, had left India.

"He was the most beautiful thing that ever existed on earth," Lady L. said, drying her eyes. "I have lived another sixty years, looking at men's faces, just because

I hoped, sometime, to catch a resemblance, a trace. But, of course, this could not be. God made in him his masterpiece, even if the masterpiece didn't believe in God. Oh, well, maybe I'm still in love. Maybe it was only my eyes that saw such beauty in him. I don't know and I don't care. But from then on, from that very first look, I knew there would never be another man for me—that nothing else would ever matter or exist."

Sir Percy was sitting there, his hands crossed over his walking stick. The two dark swans were gliding slowly between the water lilies. The air was sweet and insects were darting over the pond, among the trembling butter-flies.

CHAPTER FOUR

Lady L. remained silent for a while, closing her eyes. She was thinking how very fortunate she had been, how very lucky: she could have been born a lady, like so many of her friends, or simply into a good home and a happy family, and then she would not have found herself in that small room in the Rue de Furcy and she would never have known how beautiful life could be. Then she spoke in a voice that sounded so young and so girlish that Sir Percy, who didn't even look at her, stirred uneasily on the marble seat and cleared his throat.

"It's no good regretting the past," she said. "He was the first lovely thing I had ever seen and my life had been so ugly. I stared and stared at him, not listening to what he was saying and just smiling and feeling that I knew suddenly why I was born. I just couldn't take my eyes away from him. I suppose I have an artistic nature —let's leave it at that. All that I can say is that I am now more than sixty years older than I was then and I have spent all those years alone, looking at all the beauty that the world has to offer, from Carpaccio to Giotto, from Capri to the Valley of the Kings, trying to find something that will fill the void. . . . But to this day, I have found nothing. I fell in love, and that was that— forever."

She fell silent again and pressed her hand across her eyes.

Sir Percy sat motionless, leaning over his stick. "What happened then?" he mumbled gruffly.

Lady L. repressed a smile. It was just like good old Silly to ask what happened *then*.

It took Annette very little time to understand what sort of man the revolutionary was, and when, years later, in his *Anatomy of Anarchy*, Boremin described Armand Denis as "naïve," Lady L., when she read that description, gave it her wholehearted, if secret, approval. She began to listen carefully as he went on speaking in the same breath of justice and of murder, of love for mankind and of destruction and she was quick to recognize the words, the theme: she had listened to them before. But the very things she had hated so deeply in her father, she now felt ready to worship in Armand. With an instinctive intelligence and truly feminine cunning, she instantly applied herself to appear to the dark angel who was preaching the gospel of revolt such as he wanted her to be. She was determined to conquer him from the very first moment she saw him, and so she used all her wits to appear to him as an indignant and exploited soul, a victim of the hated *bourgeoisie,* eager to share his life and his struggles. Oh, yes, she knew everything about anarchism: her father had taught her a lot about it and he had given his life for his beliefs. She was only twelve when she first started to help him, carrying subversive literature in her laundry basket about the streets. She lied with such conviction and fitted herself so easily into her part that she ended almost believing it herself, and when, a few weeks later, she took Armand to her father's grave, she cried sincerely and was truly moved.

While Annette spoke about herself, eager to convince and please, the young man listened with a smile of almost childish ecstasy. Wasn't this an extraordinary coincidence that they should have met? His good luck had led to him the ideal accomplice, the very person who could best understand him and help him in his mission. But no, luck did not exist; it was not a mere chance, an accident of fate, that had brought them together; it was simply a proof that his ideals were beginning to spread and to take root in the hearts of the masses. Soon they will fill the world with their triumphant voices. Soon . . . He stood there, looking like the print of the young Bonaparte that Annette had seen on the wall of a Corsican café in the Rue de Lappe, and his vibrant voice was so moving and convincing that she began to cry. He was talking now of universal love. Universal love was the last thing she cared about—all she wanted was to touch his eyes, his cheek, to caress his hair. But she played her part with such feeling and conviction that Armand was overjoyed and exultant at the thought that he had found the perfect comrade at last. And when, with tears streaming down her cheeks—sincere tears, for she had never been so deeply moved—she told him that she would gladly give her life for the cause, he took her in his arms—and that was all she wanted. She raised her

78

hand and touched his lips gently and smiled—the first completely innocent and gay smile of her life. Nothing in what she had learned in her daily contacts with men had prepared her for this part, yet somehow, perhaps because her emotions were sincere, she felt instantly at ease in it, finding the right words, the right attitude. She was putting a very cold and determined mind to the service of a passionate and tender heart.

Thus they spent together the deepest hour of the night, sitting side by side on the bed, holding hands and talking of revolt, and Annette was surprised by the strange innocence and restraint of the suddenly apprehensive and almost embarrassed youth, and even more by her own shyness and trembling—and then she found the courage at long last to close his lips with her mouth, and until dawn found them there was nothing but the first and overwhelming discovery of happiness. When they came down into the café again, they found Krajewski asleep on the green sofa, the jockey dozing in a chair, erect, his eyes closed, a pistol in his lap. Lecoeur was gone. Armand woke the pianist and took him to his hotel. Before leaving, Krajewski looked at Annette with wonder.

"I will never have such a beautiful girl again in my audience," he said, and he was to repeat this, a little nostalgically, in his own written account of the adventure.

He was wrong.

A few years before his death, after a concert he had given at Lady L.'s house, the virtuoso was seated at the right hand of his hostess. He did not recognize her, which irritated Lady L. not a little.

It was already a triumph for Annette that, during the days that followed, Armand hardly talked to her about his plans. It was she herself who, very astutely, knowing that in the end she would be judged by him on her devotion to the cause and not to her lover, brought up the matter again. Armand looked a little embarrassed for having indulged, if only for a few days, in personal happiness and began to explain what was expected from her. He was going to set up a new Anarchist International in Switzerland and they needed help. He and Lecoeur had been looking everywhere for a beautiful and dedicated girl who could gain entrance to the houses of the rich and help them in a series of well-planned robberies. A young, beautiful girl would hardly be thought of as a member of an anarchist group and thus would be able to move freely, gather information, help them from the inside and be of invaluable assistance to the movement. It was, of course, essential that she should remain above suspicion and that she should live therefore as a member of the privileged class. They were already planning their first coup, which was the assassination of Michael of Bulgaria, who had suppressed the uprising of starving peasants in his native land and then gone on to Switzerland to admire the landscape. A Bulgarian comrade was to be entrusted with the task, but the actual preparations were the responsibility of the movement.

Lady L. suddenly heard, loud and clear, a very strong oath come from the lips of Sir Percy Rodiner. It was almost like a bark and for one moment, as she looked at him, the Poet Laureate appeared as determined, furious and menacing as all those well-beloved leaders of the empire whom the cartoonists of *Punch* represent as bulldogs.

"Now, that was very rude of you, Percy, dear," she said.

"Damn it, damn it, damn it, Diana!" Sir Percy roared. "Do you mean that you actually had something to do with a man who planned to kill the Grand Duke Michael of Bulgaria? Why, damn it, he was a cousin of the Marymounts! Do you realize that you will never be received at Court if this thing gets to be known? I don't

care if you were a woman of the streets, as you claim—
anyway, it happened in France, so what can you expect?
—but what I want to know is, did you truly have something to do with a regicide?"

"What do you mean, something to do with him?" Lady
L. asked. "I had *everything* to do with him."

She was beginning to feel quite worried for Percy.
The poor dear old thing was positively frothing at the
mouth.

"Damn it, you know perfectly well that the Grand
Duke Michael *was* actually murdered by a Bulgarian in
Geneva . . ."

"Naturally," said Lady L. with satisfaction. "We
planned it very carefully."

"What do you mean, 'we'?" Sir Percy roared.

"Armand, Lecoeur, the jockey, and myself—who
else?" Lady L. said. "And I really must beg you not to
shout, Percy. It's bad manners."

"Bad manners be—" Sir Percy caught himself in
time, but his whole head began to shake so violently that
flakes of dandruff wafted down onto his shoulders. Lady
Diana leaned forward and brushed them off almost lovingly.

"Do you realize that one of your grandsons is a Cabi-

net Minister?" Sir Percy roared. "That James is sitting
on the Board of the Bank of England? That Anthony is
soon to be a bishop? And you want me to believe that
their grandmother, one of the most revered, admirable
women of our time, whose portraits by Lavery, Whistler
and Sargent were in the Royal Academy, has taken part
in a regicide?"

"Well, you don't have to tell them," Lady L. remarked, a little regretfully. "Though I must say it would
be *rather* fun."

Sir Percy inhaled deeply, trying to regain control of
himself.

"Diana," he said, in a low, slightly trembling voice,
"I must ask you for a straight answer. Did you take part
in the assassination of a cousin of the Marymounts, who,
as you well know, are related to our own Royal Family?"

"Yes, of course I did," Lady L. said firmly. "We
had to draw the plan very carefully. Tovaroff, the assas-
sin, was a complete fool, although well-meaning, and he
just sat there in his hotel room, with his dagger out,
trembling and muttering, and we had to keep him locked
up most of the day. I had found out from Count Raut-
lich at what time the Grand Duke Michael would be
driving from the station and I remember that I was so

scared that I went to church and burned a candle to the Holy Virgin so that everything would go well. Then I rushed back to the Hotel des Princes, where Armand, Alphonse Lecoeur and the jockey had arranged seats on the balcony so that we could watch the assassination through our opera glasses.

"I was late and it almost began without me. I rushed to the balcony and sat on a gold-and-white Louis the Sixteenth chair and I remember Armand handing me the glasses so I could watch it all better. I still had the *Almanach de Gotha* and *Burke's Peerage* in my hands, because Armand had insisted that I should study them carefully and I had been at it all the day. We had moved into the best hotel in town the day before, so that no one would suspect us if Tovaroff got caught or talked to the police. I sat there, it seemed to me for hours, eating *marrons glacés*—they always had the best *marrons glacés* in Switzerland—but I suppose it was only a matter of minutes before the carriage drew in front of the hotel and Tovaroff rushed from the crowd and stabbed the Grand Duke through the heart. He did so twice, too. Very Bulgarian, isn't it? I didn't like it, although I must say that Michael *had* been awfully naughty; he had butchered literally thousands and thousands of peasants, who protested because they were hungry. But there was nothing that could be done about it and, seen through the lorgnette, it looked very much like opera."

Sir Percy Rodiner now appeared stricken to the point of fatal collapse. His chin touched his chest and he was holding his head in both hands. The light of the English afternoon—a measured light that never dared to insist—polite, restrained and well bred—made Lady L. long suddenly for some splash of violent color, coarse, splendid, arrogant and rude. She hated gentility. Seen from the distance, on the bench under the chestnut trees, they probably looked, she thought, like an old couple waiting for the brush of an Impressionist master. She had never really liked Impressionists, although the house was full of them. It seemed to her that they lacked passion. Then Sir Percy lifted his head and looked so pitifully toward her, his poor blue eyes were so pathetic, that she felt sorry for him. But she needed his help and so he had to know.

"You are only teasing me, Diana. Teasing me has always been your favorite sport in life. You have invented the whole story just because you know how attached I am to the Marymounts—why, I was staying with them only last week. It's all an absolute fabrication, but I must admit that I was taken in for a while . . ."

Lady L. got up and gently touched his arm.

"Come on, Percy, you need a drink. Let's walk to the pavilion. If you still don't believe me, you will see it with your own eyes. It's all there."

CHAPTER FIVE

*L*ady L. always remembered the next few months with a slight shudder. It had seemed to her at times that helping her mother with the laundry or accepting "visitors" in her lodgings was nothing compared to the torture of trying to become a lady. From morning until night, under the supervision of Armand himself and with a series of different tutors, she was taught how to walk, how to sit, how to eat, how to look, how to dress, how to move, even how to breathe, and although Armand kept repeating lovingly that poise was natural to her, that she couldn't do wrong, that it was only a matter of acquiring a very superficial polish, she often broke down and sobbed over her exercise books, covered, under the instruction of Monsieur Poupat, the state calligrapher, with elegant *A*s, *B*s and *C*s; handwriting was then considered very important and she was taught it relentlessly several hours a day.

"You will have to write many a *billet doux* to your aristocratic suitors," Armand told her, "and as I shan't always be there to dictate them for you, you'll have to master this little art yourself."

Fortunately for Annette, those first years of "indoctrination" by her father, those endless hours she had spent reading aloud to him chapters from Proudhon and from Louis Blanc, learning by heart and then reciting to her contented parent the most inspired pages of the prophets of social revolt, had not been in vain; she learned quickly and well. Presently she was moved into an elegant apartment near the Palais Royal, under the name of Mademoiselle de Cuvigny, a young lady from the provinces who had come to Paris in the hope of shining in the theater. There it was that the retired matinée idol of the Comédie-Française, Monsieur de

Tully, penniless, forgotten and suffering from a chronic throat disease, which reduced the once famous voice that had filled theaters with echoes of Racine and Corneille to a tragic murmur, was called upon to give her lessons in those *tableaux vivants* which she was expected to play later to perfection, not on the stage, but in real life.

The old actor, who was unaware of the true motives behind those lessons in *maintien,* would often exclaim, showing off *cette prodigieuse enfant* to Armand, who was watching the performance closely: *"Elle est formidable!* Natural gifts, natural poise. Genius, born to touch all hearts. Mademoiselle, you will become a famous actress under my tuition. I guarantee complete success."

The most difficult thing was to get rid of that strong, unmistakable Parisian accent of the streets, which was so much part of her voice that nothing seemed able to overcome it. And then, the vocabulary—how *not* to use certain words, how to use others—and the heartbreaking, terrorizing, agonizing discovery of propriety. After all the ugly facts of life she had been taught so early in life, she was now introduced to polite literature, to the *bibliothèque rose,* and, after having first learned to read by pages from the *Principles of Anarchy,* she was now introduced to the fables of La Fontaine and virtuous tales considered suited to young ladies. Her taste for

beauty was instinctive and it began to help her with
manners, with poise, and it soon led her to the discovery
that living was a question of style. Then came the most
delicate and the most unexpected part of her education.
She had learned too much from men who were in a
hurry, quick and precise in their desires, and Armand,
with all the tenderness he could muster, told her that she
had to be less direct, that she had to learn how to show
herself more reserved, more ignorant and shy. She had
to learn to be *maladroite* and that would pass for innocence well enough. . . .

Sir Percy Rodiner suddenly stopped in his tracks,
took the handkerchief from his pocket and wiped his
face. He tried to speak but only a grunt came from his
lips and he just stood there in the middle of the path,
under the chestnut trees, his head shaking, leaning
heavily on his stick.

"What is it now?" Lady L. asked sharply. "You really
must try to be a little more worldly, Percy."

The Poet Laureate gave her an injured look but said
nothing. There was a sound of voices and quick, patter-
ing footsteps behind them: her great-grandchildren were
running toward them. There were three of them; the
little boy, Patrick, in his Eton jacket, was carrying her

coat and he looked pleased and important to have been entrusted with such a mission. They stopped in front of the couple and stood there in respectful silence. There is no denying that the children were brought up properly, Lady L. thought. They had manners.

"I am bringing you your coat, Granny," the little boy said. "Mummy is quite worried about you. It's getting chilly."

Lady L. smiled lovingly. She had a weakness for the little boy. He was charming and, anyway, she had always preferred little boys to little girls.

"Thank you, Patrick, dear," she said. "Will you please take it back to Mummy and tell her not to worry; I'm quite all right. At my age, there is nothing to worry about, anyway."

"You are not so old, Granny," the little boy said, comfortingly. "Mummy says that you will live to be a hundred."

"What a perfectly *horrible* idea," Lady L. said. "Now run along. We are having a little chat, Sir Percy and I. Isn't that so, Percy?"

The Poet Laureate cleared his throat and emitted a series of sounds, among which the words "quite all right" managed finally to find their way out.

The children obeyed instantly, as they always did.

"Sweet little things," Lady L. said. "So well brought up. Yes, everything had gone rather well—according to plan, as the military say. Come on, Percy dear. We are almost there."

After the initial six months of heartbreaking difficulties, Annette began to learn so quickly that Armand made an error which almost ended in catastrophe. He had decided to put Annette's aptitude to test by sending her to a famous finishing school, a *pension de jeunes filles* in the Rue Monceau, where young girls from good families spent a year between the convent and marriage. After the first few weeks of *bon ton*, as old Mademoiselle de Fusigny, the head of the institution, was reading aloud a particularly tearful passage from *Paul and Virginie*, Annette, overcome with boredom, was suddenly heard saying through her teeth, but with appalling clarity, and in an unmistakable voice of the *faubourg*, "*Oh, là, là, c'qu'on s'emmerde ici!*" It ran through the classroom with such devastating sincerity and clarity that there could not be any doubt left in Mademoiselle's mind that the young lady was not at all what she pretended to be. She soon found out from other girls that Annette referred to her as "*Cette vieille maquerelle.*" She made rapid inquiries and discovered that the

different sponsors given by the "uncle" of the new pu-
pil were nonexistent. The police were called in to find
out if a burglary was afoot, but fortunately Annette had
been warned of Mademoiselle's suspicions by one of the
pupils who had nothing but admiration for her vocabulary and for the unmistakably firsthand experiences she
had in certain interesting matters. Annette had managed
to escape before the arrival of Monsieur le Commissaire,
though not without leaving behind a note, written in a
very elegant hand, but in such language that the director
of the finishing school clutched at her heart, and then
fainted outright. On being revived, the mere recollection
of the black sheep that had managed to mingle un-
suspected for several weeks among her gentle flock
caused her to faint again.

At that time the affairs of Alphonse Lecoeur and of
his companions had taken their final and disastrous turn.
In the memoirs of Commissaire Gallien, it is stated
rather cynically that Lecoeur would probably have died
peacefully in his bed, respected by all, had he not tried
to give a social meaning to his crimes and had he been
content to remain quietly and modestly the procurer and
blackmailer he had been for twenty years of his life.
Thus it was that Annette's education had been cut short
and that she found herself in Switzerland, in a new and

completely different world. Lecoeur's bitterness was immense as he sat brooding on the terrace of a café in Lausanne, presented by Armand to various Russian nihilists and Italian anarchists as a revered freedom fighter, while the jockey, with his sad, narrow face and strangely twisted head, looked at his friend with his reproachful, devoted eyes.

CHAPTER SIX

Their first weeks together in Switzerland left Annette with such a feeling of happiness that it made Lady L. feel that she had had, after all, a happy childhood. Even the loaded pistols that Armand always kept by his bedside did not convey any thoughts of danger, for those were moments stronger than any fear.

She was living alone at the Hotel des Bergues with a forged passport, the still grieving young widow of the

Count de Sudery—but every day, she would climb to the
fourth floor of a house in the old part of Geneva and
there throw herself silent, breathless, and at home, at
last, into his arms. Leaning over her "black swan," as
she called him, as close to each other as the narrow
student's bed wanted them to be, in the room filled with
books, newspapers, manuscripts and burned-out candles,
her hair streaming over her breast, she would follow
with her finger the expression of almost childish happiness on his face, as if to pin it down and to keep it
there forever. For several weeks it looked as if a sweet
adolescent had come up from the dark depths where he
had been submerged so long and the two loaded pistols
lying by the bedside had been left behind by a terrorist
who had departed forever. Forgotten were the big words,
the great conspiratorial schemes, the kings to be killed,
the bridges to be blown up, the pamphlets to be printed,
and the only thing that remained in her arms was a
young man in love. No doubt, *Liberté*, *Egalité*, and
Fraternité were waiting somewhere outside, impatiently
pacing the streets, furious, frustrated, and looking at
their watches. But she was much too feminine to think
about the future.

Then they would get up and go out on the balcony and
look over the roofs of the old town of Geneva, at the

pale waters of the great lake that seemed to carry in them the suggestion of everything that was calm, smiling and contented in the world.

"I wish I knew a love song."

"Haven't you learned any, Annette?"

"I don't care for the ones I know; they aren't happy enough. Why is it that they make all love songs so sad and so short? The poets who write them must be either tubercular or short of breath, or stupid. Armand, you have written books. Why don't you write a love song?"

"I will try. It might be a welcome change from my usual literary vein and it will be a tribute to a fleeting moment of happiness. . . ."

And that was how the anonymous song, so popular in the late eighties in France, "To a Fleeting Moment of Happiness," was written and later put to music by Aristide Fillol, and when one day Lady L. heard it in the streets of Paris for the first time, and recognized the words—*"Adieu, moment furtif, bonheur humain qui passe"*—tears came to her eyes and she hid her face in her hand. For Armand Denis had not succeeded any better than all the other poets before him: he had made his love song very short and much too sad.

But *Liberté, Egalité,* and *Fraternité* were getting impatient and soon made her feel their presence again.

More and more often, after having run quickly up the stairs, she would find the door locked and some mysterious-looking man would open it for her. Armand was constantly offering refuge to anarchists in hiding, rebellious Poles, terrorist Germans who were forever bungling their attempts to kill the Kaiser, or Hungarians, still telling of Kossuth. They were either sharing his room, sleeping on the floor, or just meeting there and holding endless discussions on how to stop man's government by man, how to suppress authority, how to destroy the State which seemed to them the bitter enemy of all human freedom. They were all strong individualists and, thinking of themselves as precursors, they were, in fact, the last survivors of the strongly individualistic romantic age of which Nietzsche was himself both a prophet and a victim and which was to find in the twentieth century its last decadent expression in Fascism. They burned with bright, destructive fire in the last twenty years of the nineteenth century, killing French presidents, Russian czars, Italian kings, throwing bombs in parliaments and filling the courts with their inspired eloquence before walking proudly to the guillotine.

Ravachol, whom Paris newspapers called the "Prince of Darkness," Vaillant, who threw a bomb in the French parliament, Henry, who blew up a fashionable café, the

childish-looking Santo Caserio, who stabbed to death
the President of the French Republic—those were the
famous ones, but there were many others. Annette was
forever finding them in the little room, grouped around
pieces of cheese, bread or sausage spread on a greasy
paper on the table. One of them lay in hiding there for
two weeks, a bearded, bald, fat Russian, who smelled of
tobacco from head to foot and who was waiting for
money from his mother so that he could go back to
St. Petersburg and assassinate the Czar of Russia. He
spoke of his mother constantly, explaining what a generous, extraordinary, intelligent and superior woman she
was. His name was Kovalski and his mother was the
famous Countess Kovalski, who had been deported to
Siberia for her sympathies with the revolutionaries. A
few weeks later, Kovalski did go back to Russia, but instead of blowing up the Czar, he inadvertently blew up
his own mother in an accident with a homemade bomb.
There was Malikoff, a young Russian ex-officer, a former
member of the Czar's own Corp des Pages, a silent,
withdrawn man who sat there playing chess endlessly
against himself, and always losing. And Napoleon Ros-
setti, an extremely jovial, cheerful little Italian from
Padua, very frivolous and gay, who walked about
Geneva with six bombs in his briefcase:

"One never knows, Mademoiselle," he explained to Annette, "whom one might meet on the lovely shores of Lake Leman; my motto is: Ever ready."

In her library, Lady L. had the best collection of books on the nineteenth-century anarchists and she often allowed students and writers to study them. It had remained her favorite reading to this day, and as she lay there in her bed, among the paintings of Tiepolo, Boucher, Fragonard, she remembered faces, the inflamed oratory, the noble gestures. But how pathetic and old-fashioned those once-feared men seemed to her now! They still belonged to the craftsman's age when everything was done by hand and it was fortunate, she thought, that they didn't live long enough to get at the atom bombs.

The little group around Armand Denis in Geneva was then in full revolt against the trends of contemporary revolutionary thinking. They hated Bakunin and Kropotkin, but above all they hated Karl Marx and the socialists, whom they considered their archenemies. They listened to Armand's torrents of passionate eloquence with the deepest respect and approval and they all had the extraordinary ability to go hungry for days without ever lessening their flow of talk.

After Annette's first few encounters with the group,

Armand had laid down the rule that she was to avoid coming to him when his room was thus occupied by "guests." Her anonymity was essential for the success of his plans, and so, when the comrades were around, she was not allowed to meet him—and for this she hated them even more.

She was then left very much on her own and consoled herself with an enjoyment of everything her new life had to offer. She loved to be driven in an open carriage through the Swiss countryside, with only her parasol between her and the sky. Looking at the romantic villas with their mysterious balconies, watching a polite game of croquet played on the lawn by beautifully dressed ladies and distinguished-looking gentlemen, visiting the gardens of the Villa Borghese, where a guide had to be hired to lead the visitor through the maze of flowers and exotic trees, of picturesque rocks, and ponds and Japanese midget forests, she wanted desperately to be rich, to own a house, to drive in her own carriage, to walk among her own flowers. It seemed to her that flowers were the luxury of the earth. She would talk to gardeners, learn the names of plants and, closing her eyes, try to recognize the fragrance of each flower and call it by its name, and when her guess was right, she would feel that she had made a new and lifelong friend.

Lecoeur still had enough gold to provide her with all the weapons of luxury which she needed to play her part effectively. She loved to look at herself standing in front of a mirror in a new hat, playing with a new boa around her shoulders, a tulle veil adding mystery to her face, while the shop attendants would exclaim, *"Que mademoiselle est donc belle!"*

She liked to sit in tearooms and listen to the ladies chattering in French, Russian or German around her, while some thin, long-haired Italian would play his violin and his fat companion would sing *"O Sole Mio,"* pressing a hairy hand against his heart. She was succeeding so well in looking a lady that none of the lonely elderly gentlemen who explored the tearooms ever ventured to address her. Then sometimes a quick, daring glance would dart through the refined atmosphere, a look of such gaiety and amusement that one almost feared it would smash the china, and before the surprised gentlemen would have time to wonder, or to presume, her lips would severely suppress the beginning of an impudent smile, a distant, ladylike expression would be back again and the words of Monsieur de Tully would ring perfunctorily in her ears:

"Remember, *mon enfant*. . . . You are distant . . . you are unapproachable . . . you are inaccessible. . . .

You are a goddess, alone on your Olympus. . . . No one must dare, no one must presume. . . . You can only be revered and respectfully admired from a distance. . . ."

And then again the quick look of gaiety and something like the promise of a smile—and once more, before any of the bewildered admirers could believe their eyes, there would be no other expression on her face but that of beauty—the lovely, firm nose, the perfectly designed lips, the truly aristocratic features and those heavy eyelashes that seemed to palpitate under the weight of their own modesty.

She loved to visit jewelers' shops and to look at the fine Italian cameos, then the epitome of fashion—Lady L. still had boxes and boxes of them—or try on earrings, bracelets, and brooches, and it was indeed a tribute to her will power and to her newly acquired respectability that she never stole anything, although the temptation was sometimes so great that she could almost have wept. She soon discovered that luxury did not stop at manmade things. The whole earth was an explosion of riches, of color, of brilliance, of fragrance, that no goldsmith, jeweler or perfumer could ever hope to match. She had a natural eye for beauty. She instinctively knew how to recognize *"le vrai chic"* from mere *"tape à l'oeil,"* the perfect design from loud attempts to catch the eye, and how to add to her toilette the final, almost imperceptible touch that made her instantly the best-dressed woman in any elegant crowd.

She was learning more from her contact with nature than from all that she had been so painstakingly told by Monsieur de Tully. A branch of lilac was a lesson in grace; watching swans gliding proudly on the lake, looking at flowers, she suddenly knew more about poise than from all the manuals of comportment; and very soon, sitting at Rumpelmayer's, listening to the discreet chatter of polyglot voices or looking at the paintings at some fashionable *vernissage,* she began to attract everybody's attention, by that natural something which the astute aristocrats of many lands could not fail to recognize as true nobility—that unmistakable quality, as they told each other knowingly, that cannot be acquired except through generations of pure breeding. Years later, remembering the first impression she had made on her admirers, Lady L. would often throw back her head and laugh. And when the painters exclaimed at her style and carriage, she would say gaily, "Well, it can all be learned from flowers."

She became very fond of music. Her ear was quick at distinguishing a true virtuoso from a mere performer, and as she sat in the concert audience, her eyes half closed and a smile on her lips—the famous smile of Lady L. that was still there at the age of eighty—she decided that the voluptuous luxury of music was second only to that of love. But she was never to lose her weakness for a *valse musette* or even a *java,* though they were considered then as much too vulgar. But in later years, she felt sure enough of herself to like what she liked, and it was she who set the standards.

Armand and the group were beginning to need money. There were so many people to help, the secret printing press to be installed, young students to be indoctrinated and trained, political exiles from all countries to be helped, and finally the great plan—"insurrection by deeds"—to be put into action. The only way to get the necessary means was by robbery, and Annette was going from one rich villa to another, sipping tea, playing croquet, listening to chamber music in elegant drawing rooms, and wondering which was the house that ought to be robbed first.

She had established the necessary contacts through the good offices of a certain Baron de Beren. The Baron was one of those unfortunate souls whom Alphonse Lecoeur had been blackmailing for years and whom he held entirely in his power through the old aristocrat's fatal weakness for danger; long ago he had discovered that he couldn't enjoy his pleasures unless they were taken on the brink of the abyss and in the imminence of a deadly fall. And if the elegant, slender, gray-haired aristocrat, buried in his heavy fur coat, monocle shining in his terrified yet delighted face, had never had his throat cut on one of his dangerous slumming expeditions, he owed this to the long and powerful arm of Lecoeur. It was de Beren who played chaperon to Annette among the wealthy, pleasant and politely bored society of Geneva. He had been brought especially to Switzerland for that purpose, under several severe threats. He didn't want to come: he hated nature, and above all the pure Swiss air. But he knew better than to disobey. He came to Switzerland and fell ill immediately—an asthma attack. He always suffered from asthma when placed under healthful conditions. It took him several weeks to establish the young Countess Diane de Sudery firmly in the circle of his rich friends, and then he rushed back to Paris and his dark *folies*. But his apache protector was no longer there to shield him, and a few months later his body was found in the gutter near the Bastille, his face still wearing an expression of terrified delight.

Annette had moved easily into that charmed circle of

the wealthy, leisurely, socially unconcerned, "happy few" who drifted like some migratory birds from one season to another, from opera to ballet, from spa to spa, taking the waters in Baden-Baden or Kissingen, picnicking on the shores of pleasant lakes or under the snow-capped mountains, while their daughters, guarded by the strictest governesses England could provide, painted graceful water colors in the manner of Edward Lear and dreamed at the piano. Switzerland was then the favorite playground of those prudent travelers to whom Mont Blanc was still the most awe-inspiring sight; the Victorian age, in its full plushy bloom, had established its most advanced outposts on the shores of Como, Stresa and Garda. But among these apparently blasé and restricted Victorians, Annette had met one of the most truly sophisticated and cultivated men of his time.

The Duke of Glendale, "Dicky" to his friends, was then in his sixties and for years he had been Queen Victoria's pet aversion. His enemies considered him corrupt; his friends saw him as an embodiment of wisdom. His eccentricity was famous, an eccentricity that was his own peculiar form of revolt. He had probably inherited it from his father, who had accompanied Lord Byron on his ill-fated expedition to Greece, not, as he took care to explain, because he cared about Greek independence, but because he had always regretted that he had not been there to listen when Nero fiddled while Rome burned, and he was sure that in flaming Greece, Byron's fiddle would find some of its most beautiful harmonies. After the poet's death, he went on to fight on the side of Ypsilanti, risking his life several times to capture Mount Hillios from the Turkish Army, and when the enemy finally retreated, he had proceeded to remove from the temple of Hillios every single piece of statuary that could be transported. Victory thus achieved, he had returned triumphantly to England with his treasures.

His son had married a gypsy, to the horror of the young queen and her court, and after his wife had died, he went to live for several years with her tribe in Spain. His taste became legendary among the art dealers and museum curators of the world; he saw in art the only and true form of revolt accessible to man, a true "insurrection by deed," a rebellion against his own mortality, against his frailty, and, above all, against ugliness. His tolerance and benevolence appeared to many merely a supreme form of indifference; his impatience with the accepted values and conventions and also his mordant wit had made it all but impossible for him to live in England.

He had shown an immediate interest in Annette and, though obviously attracted by her, had not overlooked something strange in her manner. With his narrow, faintly Oriental eyes, high cheekbones and that smile permanently settled in the corners of the mouth, with his retinue of French cooks, Italian major-domos, Irish horse trainers, with his special train carrying him wherever he desired to go, the best racing stables, the best dogs, the greatest private collection of Renaissance art— he was somehow completely detached from it all, looking at his own happiness and fortune as one more proof of the indiscriminate absurdity of life.

Almost imperceptibly, Annette began learning from him attitudes, mannerisms, a certain quizzical way to look at the world, which were to mark her deeply and forever. He had never asked her any questions about her past, and although his very avoidance of the subject was perhaps a sign of a certain suspicion, in his presence she never felt self-conscious or embarrassed. She didn't care if she made a *faux pas*, if the accent of the streets of Paris suddenly appeared in her speech, or if a word of slang slipped out. But for all the pleasure she found in his company, she did not neglect her task and made a careful plan of the house and its treasures, with each showcase and its contents clearly marked. She did it day by day during the sketching séances they held on the terrace of the villa. Glendale was making a drawing of her, while Annette herself, holding her sketching block on her knee, pretended to be drawing the statue of Apollo standing in the garden.

"Tell me, Dicky, what are those marvelous little objects on the second floor, to the right in the corridor, just before the entrance to the library?"

One eye closed, Glendale was measuring her with the pencil he held in his outstretched hand.

"They are Egyptian golden scarabs. They were specially stolen for me from a Pharaoh's tomb. As a matter of fact, I have a permanent team of archaeologists stealing for me in Egypt. I hope to have the head of the expedition knighted this year. They have discovered a new tomb and they are engaged in robbing it for me right now."

"Are those lovely little things very valuable?"

"Priceless."

Annette lifted Apollo on his page and marked the position of the showcase on the page beneath it. She wrote in the margin: "Egyptian golden scarabs. Very valuable."

"As a matter of fact, I might go to Egypt myself

next spring," Glendale said. "How would you like to come with me?"

"I would love to. But please, Dicky, about those scarabs—just for curiosity's sake—if you were selling them, how much would you ask?"

"The Louvre has offered me five thousand pounds apiece, but Kaiser Wilhelm, who stayed here with me last year, offered almost double and didn't get them."

"Ten thousand apiece?" Annette asked, lowering her voice respectfully, for she still had a sound respect for money. "Do you think he would really pay that much?"

"He would be delighted to do so. I wouldn't even be surprised if he started a war with England just to get these scarabs away from me."

Annette wrote down the sum, dutifully underlined, and noted the name of the prospective purchaser, Kaiser Wilhelm of Germany. She wondered suddenly if she couldn't confide her secret to her new friend; Dicky was broad-minded enough to understand, and to approve and perhaps even to help her to rob himself. He had told her once that the most important thing in life was love and that all the rest was nothing. Her almost childish admiration for him was such that she was unable to hide it from Armand, and the young anarchist was dismayed and angry.

"He's a selfish sybarite who cares for nothing but his own pleasure!" he exclaimed. "I've had enough of that so-called sophisticated attitude which sees in cynicism and skepticism a form of wisdom. His whole way of life is an insult to humanity. He is a typical product of a corrupt age. You ought to know better, Annette. He has retreated into the world of art so as not to see all the ugliness, the slavery and the poverty that are staring him in the face."

"But he's so generous and kind," Annette tried to argue. "He supports hundreds of artists, musicians, writers. . . . They would have starved without him, or accomplished nothing."

"I don't doubt it," Armand said sarcastically. "The artist in our time is an accomplice of the ruling classes. His creations are used as an opium for the people. The ruling classes hope to send the masses to museums, as they used to send them to churches, to make them forget their wretchedness. The poets who sing songs to the people, the painters who throw a veil over reality, the musicians who try to make us forget—those are our great enemies. Your friend is a clever and dangerous reactionary."

They were walking through a field on Mont Pelerin, overlooking Geneva and the shores of France. The white mountains towered like gigantic sailboats over the humble white butterflies that skimmed so lightly over the lake. It was narcissus season—and the narcissi grew so thick that Annette, her arm around Armand, smiled, thinking that she wouldn't mind at all being kept with him forever a prisoner of the flowers.

"Your disgusting friend is rotten to the core, completely amoral, and his only purpose in life is the pursuit of pleasure," Armand concluded.

Annette sighed; she knew of no more worthy pursuit. If only Armand were a little amoral, she thought, if only his sole purpose in life could be the pursuit of pleasure—how happy they could have been together! It was not so much that she minded robbing the Glendale collection, but it seemed such a shame to throw away all this fortune on blowing up bridges, derailing trains, killing kings, printing newspapers, supporting comrades—those comrades who never, never listened to music, noticed a landscape, or exclaimed gratefully at the beauty of a painting.

"Armand, couldn't we just once keep some of the money for ourselves, travel, see the world, be happy together? Must you always, always, give away every penny to your friends? They are such a useless lot! Naturally, I know they mean well and have high ideals. . . . But look at them! They just talk, talk, talk. . . . And what about that clumsy, tea-drinking Kovalski? All he managed to do was to blow up his own mother. Isn't that ridiculous?"

"That was an unfortunate chemical accident with nitroglycerine. He meant well."

"*Chéri,* can't we just keep a little something for ourselves? Let's rob old Dicky and then go to India, to Turkey, to Japan. . . . Just for one little year. Then we'll come back and start again. There will always be a king or a queen waiting to be killed—it's their job, after all, and they do it rather well."

Armand stared at her in amazement. This was a new Annette, a frivolous, capricious, almost a sophisticated young woman—a far cry from the frightened, embittered girl he had rescued from the streets only two years ago. He frowned, and Annette knew instantly that she had gone too far, that she had said the wrong things. After all, he was something of a priest—even if he didn't believe in God and if his code was *Liberté, Egalité, Fraternité*—and he looked the part too, a supremely handsome priest, dressed, as he always was, in black, with his burning white face and the dark eyes that seemed to carry in them the reflection of all the suffering and hope of every human being on earth. She suddenly felt scared—not of his anger, of those sudden flashes of cold fury that sometimes could be felt in his voice, but of losing him.

"Don't look at me like that," she begged. "I love you. You are my life. I will do whatever you wish. Please, please don't be angry!"

Her eyes filled with tears.

"I don't ask you to do anything for me, Annette," he told her sadly. "What you are willing to do, you must do for the people. I love you, too, there's no denying that. You are the only thing I have ever wanted for my-self. . . . But look at this happy landscape, at this smil-ing lake, at this sea of narcissi, at this clear sky: it's all a fraud. At this very moment, four fifths of humanity are dying of hunger or in chains. Remember your own childhood, think of all the children doomed the very moment they are born. . . . They look at you. They wait. Millions of slaves lift toward us their shackled hands. . . . We cannot belong to each other; we belong to them. Our happiness would be an insult to our hearts and to their suffering. Look at their starving, imploring faces. . . . Can't you see them? They are here. They are all around us. . . . Don't be fooled by flowers."

His voice shook. It carried an almost hypnotic power,

like that of his burning eyes. Annette turned her head away abruptly.

"I don't want to look at them, I don't want to!" she shouted angrily. "Please, Armand, don't make me! Please, let me see the flowers again!"

He took her in his arms.

"My poor child," he said, "it's not your fault. I am afraid that I have been a poor teacher. Your ideological education has been much too quick and I didn't devote enough time to it. I should have loved you more by teaching you more."

She sighed deeply. The only thing he had taught her was that she couldn't live without love, without him— but this, she knew, she couldn't tell him. To him, it would have sounded like blasphemy. And so only the tears streaming down her cheeks carried her true thoughts with them.

"I wish I could do more for the movement," she said humbly, with an absolute lack of conviction in her voice, but her tears were so obviously sincere that they made her words sound true. "Can't I blow up a bridge or something? Why is it that you have never asked me to throw a bomb?"

He laughed and kissed her and her relief was such that she cried with complete sincerity in his arms.

"Please, dearest, don't cry," he begged her. "You'll have plenty to do, I promise you. You are my best comrade."

"Your—what?" she sobbed, in horror.

"My best ally, my most dedicated worker. Don't be too impatient. It takes time. I promise you you will be given the same opportunity to fight for our cause as our best comrades, and your name will go down in history as that of a great fighter for human freedom."

She shook her head in despair and her sobs redoubled.

How sad, she thought, that one couldn't choose the man one loved! She would have chosen someone like Dicky, a little younger, of course. But one had no choice. One loved, and that was all.

CHAPTER SEVEN

When Annette next visited Glendale, she noticed with some annoyance that the collection of golden scarabs was gone. She inquired rather sharply what had happened to it, and Dicky looked at the empty showcase innocently.

"Oh, I had them put away in the vault. There have been some burglaries lately and I would hate to see them stolen. I can't be sure that the new owner would take good care of them. He might even melt them for gold, God forbid!"

Annette tried to look unconcerned and dignified, but somehow she was left with the unpleasant feeling that Dicky *knew*. It was quite, quite unsettling. And yet Glendale appeared more devoted to her than ever. He sought her company constantly. He taught her English, and although she never managed to lose her strong French accent, she mastered the language quickly and well. They were seen together everywhere—concerts, balls, garden parties, picnics, sailing on the lake, driving in the Swiss countryside, or over to France, on the other shore of the lake.

It was coming back from one of those long drives with her friend that Annette, after a brief but fervent stop at the church, where she burned a candle, had returned almost too late for the assassination of Michael of Bulgaria. She saw Dicky again the next day at the croquet game of Count Rodendorff, the Russian ambassador, and of course no one talked of anything else. Public opinion was outraged, and the Swiss police were severely taken to task. Conscious of the tourist trade, the Swiss authorities started a systematic check of the many exiles and political refugees, and very soon things began to look uncomfortable for Armand and his friends. They decided to move to Italy for a while, but not before carrying out the first big burglary they had planned, that of Count Rodendorff's villa.

Rodendorff was a clumsy, bearded bear of a man, famous for his extravagances, who had lost several fortunes at Monte Carlo, but still thought nothing of entertaining a hundred guests at dinner, served on gold plates. The ambassador had fallen deeply in love with the popular young Madame de Sudery and had sobbed, kneeling at her feet, when she had refused to marry him, threatening suicide, the threat that was commented upon by Glendale as "the first valuable service he would have rendered to his country." It was decided that Armand, Lecoeur and the jockey would enter the house while Annette would be attending the ballet in the company of the Russian bear. Unfortunately, the count had suddenly felt ill during the performance, from overeating, and had to be taken back to his house by his friends. Annette rushed to her hotel, trembling with apprehension. Count Rodendorff felt better on his way home and almost decided to return to the theater. His friends, however, the Russian General Dobrinski and two members of the German Embassy, insisted he should rest.

Approaching the villa, they found the door open, the servants gagged and tied, and a tall, powerful figure, with a cigar in his mouth and a pistol in his hand, standing in the hall, while another man of diminutive size was cramming gold and silver into the bags. Armand was at the moment upstairs, forcing the secretary, at pistol-point, to open the safe. Lecoeur's immediate reaction, out of sheer fury at being interrupted, was to fire at Rodendorff, wounding him in the arm. Armand, who had just finished emptying the safe, rushed downstairs, and although the trio made their exit quite easily, their description was circulated by the police everywhere and a twenty-thousand-franc reward was offered for information leading to the capture. They found themselves in dire predicament. The extraordinary good looks of Armand, the gigantic stature of Lecoeur, and the diminutive size of the jockey made it all but impossible for them to pass unnoticed. They lay low for several days in the workshop of Père Lanusse, a respected watchmaker with a fatherly pair of white mustaches, whose arrest six months later led to the discovery of enough bombs to wipe out royal Europe. The police raided the rooms occupied by Armand in the old town, and the group of Russian exiles quietly sipping tea around the samovar, together with crates of anarchist literature, were found there. It seemed only a matter of hours before Armand and his companions would be captured.

It was Annette who came to their rescue.

CHAPTER EIGHT

Annette's bedroom windows overlooked the lake. The night was passing slowly, the pale glimmer of dawn was already touching the lake; she watched anxiously every silhouette in the street, every carriage that drove by, every fisherman's boat approaching the shore. She knew that Armand was in mortal danger, yet somehow she felt certain that he was alive—for she was alive herself—that he wasn't wounded, for she felt no pain in her body.

It was only at nine o'clock in the bright, blue morning that the maid knocked at the door to tell her that a watchmaker was asking to be received.

Annette listened to the news, smoking a cigarette and pacing the room. There was only one person to whom she could turn for help, but she had to be careful, cunning, act her part well and prepare a plausible story. She knew that she was taking a risk, but it was nothing compared to the risk of losing Armand. For the first time, she was suddenly conscious that there was something almost different from love that drew her to him: a strange, half-maternal, half-tyrannical possessiveness, almost a form of avarice, a feminine and almost capricious urge to own the most desirable thing on earth. Half an hour later she had called a carriage and was on her way to see Glendale.

He was having breakfast on the balcony, sharing it with his pet toucan. It was an enormous bird, with a beak twice its size; he had acquired it in South America, and they obviously enjoyed each other's company. An elaborately encased little gold box was on the breakfast table, and as he opened it to offer her a cigarette, it played a tune. In the early-morning light, Dicky seemed older and grayer. His face had a light, petrified stillness about it, and she noticed that there were two deep lines at the corners of his mouth that must have often passed for a smile. He was wearing a Damascus robe and Turkish slippers. She wondered briefly how old the toucan was. She sat down, accepted a cigarette, and waited for the servants to leave the room.

"Dicky, the most terrible thing has happened."

"Which means that you have fallen in love, I suppose, and with the wrong man. There is, of course, no such thing as being in love with the right man."

"Dicky, there couldn't be a more completely and totally wrong man, I assure you."

"Congratulations, my dear. I'm very, very old, and I'm still looking for a completely wrong woman. They all seem to have become so terribly right."

He glanced at her.

"Well, perhaps not all of them."

"Thank you, Dicky. You are sweet. I really believe you like me."

"Can I be of any help?"

"Oh, Dicky, you don't know how impossible it is!"

"Well, who is he? A coachman? A fisherman? A waiter? A street musician? Or—God forbid—a poet?"

She began to tell her story. Not quite the true story, of course. She trusted Dicky completely, but she was still a little unsure of herself and a little ashamed of her past, and not enough of a lady to dare tell him everything. Lady L. often thought how she would have loved and enjoyed discussing it all with Dicky now, how they could have laughed together—but she wasn't yet a *grande dame* then and she couldn't afford the whole truth. That she didn't tell it then was perhaps the best proof that she still hadn't acquired that special English sophistication of the *happy few,* with its amoral, and, in a way, terroristic sense of humor, and its superior unconcern, which could lead as well to heroism as to murder. But she had prepared her story carefully and she told it well. Dicky, anyway, appeared to enjoy listening to it. The only thing that embarrassed her a little was the toucan. The bird looked at her fixedly, its head twisted to one side, and it seemed very sardonic. . . .

She had been combing her hair one evening in her hotel bedroom when she suddenly noticed that although the window was closed the red velvet curtain swayed and bulged peculiarly. She thought of ringing for the chambermaid, of course, but then something made her decide to deal with it herself. She wasn't frightened, or irritated. She walked to the curtain and there . . .

"I have never, never seen a more beautiful creature in my whole life. He was standing there in a wide-open

shirt, the pistol in his hand—the most romantic appearance you can possibly imagine. He looked a little bit
like that portrait of your friend, Lord Byron, in your
library. I wasn't frightened at all, but my heart almost
stopped. I knew instantly that he could not be a mere
burglar. That the thoughts behind that pale, pure forehead could be nothing but noble and inspired . . ."

Glendale, who was buttering his toast, winced slightly.

"It's extraordinary," he remarked. "Whenever a
woman is physically attracted by a man, she always
claims to be attracted by his soul or by his intellect.
Even when, as in your case, he obviously didn't have
time to utter a word, much less to let you admire his
noble thoughts. Confusing physical attraction with spir-
itual love is like mixing politics with idealism. Very bad.
Well, what happened next? I mean, aside from the other
thing that obviously has happened and which you seem
to have enjoyed so thoroughly."

"Please, Dicky, don't be cynical. I bandaged his
wounds—oh, yes, I forgot to tell you he was wounded.
Then I hid him in my hotel suite for several days. We
fell madly in love. After that I haven't seen him for a
week or so. Now, I'm afraid he's done something very
silly again . . ."

"Robbed that old idiot Rodendorff's house, I suppose."

"How do you know?"

"It's in the papers."

"Dicky! I'm in love."

"Who is he, exactly—aside from being irresistible?"

"I'm afraid he's an anarchist."

"Really? I find it difficult to believe from your
dreamy description. There is no such thing as a
good-looking anarchist, or socialist for that matter. They
are usually intelligent and very plain. Well, where do
we go from here?"

"He is pursued by the police. Apparently he's quite
famous. His name is Armand Denis. Did you ever hear
it before?"

For the first time since the conversation began, Glendale showed some surprise and even a trace of excitement.

"Yes, indeed I have. A romantic poet."

"He is not a poet," Annette said. "He calls himself
a social reformer. He wants to give justice, liberty—
everything—to every human being on this earth!"

"That's exactly what I say, a poet," Glendale said.
"The sort of fellow that fifty years ago would have died
of dysentery for Greek independence, as Byron did.

There is nothing more pathetic than this last debris the romantic age still keeps washing up on our almost twentieth-century shore. My friend Karl Marx has described the anarchists very well: 'Dreamers of the absolute who take their poetic inspiration for sociological doctrine.' They approach problems with an artistic longing for perfection. They sit in front of humanity as a painter sits in front of his canvas wondering how to make it a masterpiece. Instead of writing a perfect sonnet, they try to build a perfect society. Disastrous, of course. That doesn't make him a bad lover, though."

Annette looked at him pathetically. "But what am I to do? How can I help him? The whole Swiss police is after him."

"Very romantic," Glendale said, finishing his coffee. "Well, inasmuch as anything Swiss can be romantic. Why don't you go with your nice young man for a little trip to Italy and get it out of your system? That might even teach him that there are other ways to human happiness than bombs. By the way—" he reached for another piece of toast— "who are you exactly, Annette?"

Annette opened very wide her big, surprised, innocent eyes. "What do you mean? I am the Countess de Sudery."

"There has never been such a thing as a Count de

Sudery," said Glendale, looking rather bored. "However, this is beside the point. I am willing to help. Let us see . . . Where is he?"

"He is hiding in the old town. He is in terrible danger. If they catch him, they will give it to him."

Glendale couldn't help laughing at the unexpected use of Parisian underworld slang.

"They don't 'give it' to people in Switzerland, my dear," he said. "It would be much too lively. Well, I'll see what I can do. I would like to meet that young man, anyway. I have never thrown a bomb myself, but I have done my bit. In fact, I have probably, by my whole style of living, done more harm to the English aristocracy and to what your young friend probably calls 'the ruling classes' than any terrorist. I am quite ready to arrange a little romantic trip to Italy for you and your young man, my dear. It will be rather fun. I shall enjoy telling the Prince of Wales how I smuggled an anarchist out of Switzerland. I hope his respected mother will hear about it, too. It was about time that I did something for my reputation. Otherwise they might think I am losing my touch."

The escape of Armand and his friends from Switzerland was probably the most comfortable ever arranged for a man pursued by the police of three countries.

They traveled across the frontier in great style in Glendale's private train, in a carriage marked with his ducal crest. The Swiss authorities cleared the route and provided the necessary guard as, after the recent anarchist attempts, they were determined to do their best to insure the security of their most distinguished guest. Ostensibly they were taking two of the Duke's best horses for races that were to be held in Milan. The horses traveled in their stable wagon, with their groom, and with a new trainer who sported a loud checked suit and who was accompanied by a jockey who boarded the train carrying his saddle with him. Glendale and Sapper took an instant liking to each other and almost threw themselves into each other's arms: they knew the same horses.

Armand Denis came aboard immaculately dressed, offering his arm to Annette. The Swiss police provided a special guard on the train, and the Union Jack was hoisted together with the Swiss Federal flag on the station building. The conversation between the old aristocrat and the young anarchist, facing each other across the table over crystal bowls of caviar and glasses of champagne, while they waited for the chef who was attending to the pheasants and to the English sirloin, was obviously enjoyed by both parties, and Annette, although she was much more busy looking at Armand than listening to him, was very proud and pleased that her lover stood his ground so well against such an adversary. Crossing intellectual foils with one of the most brilliant men of his time, Armand showed such style, such elegance and distinction that Annette felt her anarchist lover should have been born at least an archduke.

"I can't say, Monsieur," Glendale told him, "that your logic impresses me very much. Your idea of destroying the State and then establishing order by killing off its ephemeral representatives is sadly inadequate. You overestimate the importance of the individual, be he a king or President of the Republic. Now, if you had told me that you enjoy throwing bombs as an occupation for its own sake, I could understand that, as I understand people who spend their days sitting by the edge of a lake with their fishing lines. Although, personally, I abhor fishing."

Armand shook his head in polite dissent.

"Monsieur, by killing kings, by harassing the police, by frightening the rulers, I merely intend to force the present social order to become more and more cruel in order to defend itself. The oppression will grow, and when the life of the masses becomes unendurable, they will revolt, and the whole capitalistic system will crumble into dust. Our purpose is to force society to tighten

134

its grip to the point where it will burst and destroy itself by its own excesses. We have to be excessive in order to make our enemies excessive, too. Then, when there will not be an inch of freedom left, the people will revolt and we shall win."

Glendale looked pained.

"You have a very poor idea of people, Monsieur," he said reproachfully. "I, myself, although I am an aristocrat and very, very decadent, happen to have a much higher opinion of them. They don't have to be kicked into revolt. The moment will come when, after years of watching my way of life, they will quite naturally wish to share in my pleasures. And as long as they are truly determined to enjoy life, I don't mind vanishing and being succeeded by millions of hedonists. I love pleasure. There is nothing a hedonist enjoys more than to see other people share his enjoyment of life. The true and dedicated pleasure-lover can even go without pleasure himself, provided he can enjoy the sight of other people's delight. He then becomes a *voyeur,* in the nobler sense of the word. That is perhaps the true hidden meaning of the Buddhist notion of detachment and contemplation. Buddha has reached the point when his own pleasure is no longer enough for him and he wants to be surrounded by the pleasure of millions. As long as I can hear the voice of happiness around me, I shall know contentment."

"Monsieur," Armand answered, with a slight grimace, "paradox is the typical refuge of those who know they are wrong but who will not admit their errors and mistakes, and so they try to prove that white is black and black is white."

Annette was enjoying herself thoroughly. She did not know what delighted her more—her handsome lover, with that sardonic, superior attitude of the intellectual sure of himself, or the ancient, wrinkled and tolerant hedonist who believed he knew better and whose smile hung on his lips like some ripe fruit of total wisdom.

CHAPTER NINE

During the weeks that followed, while Armand was forced to lie low in Milan, Glendale, with a conjurer's ease, revealed to Annette a new and yet infinitely ancient world. It was her first contact with Italy, and although she had expected much, she had been so little prepared for the revelation that she fell ill with excitement and had to spend several days in bed in Venice, lying on the balcony, gazing incredulously at the church of San Giorgio Maggiore across the lagoon, until the doctor, having made a correct diagnosis of her symptoms, had ordered the window closed. In Rome she had stood on the very ground where Christians were thrown to the lions, and, imagining Armand in this dire predicament, for it was obvious to her that in those days he would have been a martyr, she cried so unrestrainedly standing there in the arena that a passing priest, moved by her religious fervor and pity for the first faithful, gave her his blessing. She had looked at Rome and all the ruins, which once had been temples and palaces and had burned while Nero fiddled, and wondered if Armand, had he lived in those days, would have done the fiddling or the burning. She had driven along the Appian Way and, twirling her lace parasol, had imagined Armand as a Caesar coming back with his legions from new conquests, and then, wondering what she would have worn for the occasion, she felt an irresistible urge to go and order a new dress from Lupi, the most celebrated of the Roman couturiers. Back in Venice, gliding down the Grand Canal in Dicky's gondola, floating between his palazzo and the Fenice, visiting churches so full of beauty that it made her fall to her knees, discovering Florence and Pisa, receiving the gifts of Giotto and Carpaccio, or sitting in a box at La Scala and listening to the greatest singers, she soon decided with a sort of violent, imperious determination that this was her world, her life, her place, that this was where she belonged, here she had found her true self. Glendale watched her carefully and was delighted that his little plan was working out well.

"I'm so glad you enjoy it, my dear. There are very few people nowadays capable of real enjoyment. It takes talent truly to appreciate beauty, and you undoubtedly possess it. You must devote yourself fully to it, as a first-rate pianist devotes his whole time to practicing. You must be given all the means to develop your genius and bring it to its full maturity."

But even with all the splendors of Italy as his ally, Glendale often felt that he was fighting a losing battle, and that, whatever new discovery and excitement he could offer to Annette, love was still the only thing that mattered to her. In Milan, after a performance at La Scala, he well knew to what dark, poor corner of the town she hurried when he had kissed her hand at the door of her hotel.

"Would you like me to leave you my carriage?"

"No, darling Dicky, I will take a cab. It will be less noticeable."

He would hail a cab for her, help her in, and she would hasten to the Via Perdita where Armand was hiding in the attic of a dark and smelly house.

"How much money were you able to get today from your noble friend?" would be Armand's first words.

But she wasn't duped by this affectation of cynicism, for she knew that he resented his complete dependence on her during those weeks, when the police were still searching for him everywhere; and she was delighted to notice a trace of jealousy, almost of despair, behind his bravado. He had never needed her more and that gave her the feeling of possessing him at last. When he held her against him, pressing his face against her neck in a silent, desperate embrace, there was more truth and meaning in his deep sigh than in all his sarcastic words. Those were moments when she experienced a feeling of victory, and hope, when she felt that *Liberté, Egalité,* and *Fraternité* were loosening their grip. He needed her and so she was happy. She would lean over him, as he lay there, his head on her bare knees, her unpinned hair flowing over her bare breasts and his pale face, and she felt so gay, and so sure of keeping him to herself alone, at long last, that the eighteenth-century love song of the streets of Paris would come to her lips:

Je ne connais pas d'autre toujours
Que mon amour
Que mon amour
Je ne vivrais pas un seul jour
Sans mon amour
Sans mon amour. . . .

The Poet Laureate looked up in amazement: Lady L. was singing. She had stopped under a branch of lilac, and she was singing in French, in that strangely young voice that made him feel so uncomfortable. Her voice hadn't aged at all in all those years and it sounded almost girlish. Then suddenly the song was finished and there were tears in her eyes and on her cheeks and Sir Percy looked away unhappily.

One day, as she entered the little room with a basket of grapes, a pheasant and a bottle of wine, she found Alphonse Lecoeur and the jockey sitting on the bed, listening to Armand. He barely gave her a nod and she knew that his devouring obsession had taken hold of him again. Lecoeur, although he still looked as strong as ever, was then approaching the last stage of a well-known disease that showed itself in the size of his dilated pupils. He sat there with an expression of stupor, his face almost brick-red, and Sapper gave Annette a quick, unhappy look and lowered his eyes to his cigarette. There was another man in the little room, a baldish little Italian by the name of Marotti. They were discussing the projected assassination of King Umberto of Italy at the premiere of the new Verdi opera. Annette covered her ears and ran away. The next days followed the old, well-established pattern. She had to part with her jewels once more, and all the money went into the preparations for the attempt. The story of a pair of diamond earrings that Dicky had given her was typical of all three of them, of Annette, Glendale and Armand. The earrings were small but superb stones, beautifully set, a masterpiece of Florentine workmanship, and they dropped from her ears like burning tears of happiness. But when Armand asked for them, she had to give them up, and they were immediately sold at the Galleria. Glendale took one look at her the next evening and asked her quite sharply to whom the jewels had been sold. He then bought them back and returned them to Annette. Soon the earrings found their way to Armand once more and into the shop in the Galleria, and Glendale patiently bought them back for her. Lady L. often laughed, remembering how the same earrings had been bought back three times, and how, in spite of all her earnest promises, each time she had surrendered them to Armand once again.

In the end, Glendale became incensed. He ordered his black-and-yellow carriage with the ducal crest and was driven to Armand's hideout, which he had had under constant watch, for fear that the police might raid it while Annette was there. He walked into the little shop where Marotti worked on his printing press, and where Armand was sitting at the table writing one of those incendiary anonymous pamphlets that the Italian authorities could not pin onto any of their usual suspects. At one time they had even attributed them to D'Annunzio.

Glendale walked down the steps, took out his wallet and said sternly to Armand, "All right, how much exactly do you need to assassinate Umberto? I prefer to give you the money—but I must beg you to leave those earrings alone. She loves them. Let us consider that they are a gift from you."

The mechanism of the bomb planted in the royal box didn't work and Umberto had to wait till 1900 to be assassinated. Annette had by then discovered something about herself that she had not realized: she was fond of kings, and she wished there were more of them. She didn't care about their politics, but she liked the hush that preceded their entrance, the red carpets and the pomp, the glitter of scarlet and gold, the uniforms and the diamond-studded orders on their chests; and she only regretted that they didn't walk about with crowns on their heads and scepters in their hands: it was such good theater! She was still naïve enough to enjoy the spectacle of royalty, of white-plumed generals, or cardinals in scarlet or purple: the church dressed *so* well! There was never enough glamour and color in the world, and the kings were there for the pleasure of the eye; she didn't mind at all if they were marched to the guillotine, so long as they went there in splendid attire.

Lady L. remembered this early attitude of hers with an indulgent irony. It only went to prove that her education was not then completed, that Annette was then still far from being a lady, and that she still had in her that healthy common streak which made chambermaids and nurses pant with admiration for guardsmen, firemen, and royal bandsmen, and even policemen.

Her first effort to free herself from her love occurred later that month, just before she went with Dicky to the carnival in Venice. One night, as Annette met her lover in a closed carriage after the Princess Montanesi's ball, she noticed that Armand gave her a strange and scorn-

ful look. She had had no time to change, and her neck,
ears and wrists were glittering in the gaslight with all
the fire of emeralds and diamonds that Glendale had
lent her to wear at the ball.

They drove silently through the streets of Milan. At
first Armand stared ahead of him without a word. Then
suddenly he shouted to the coachman the name of the
poorest quarter of the city. They drove on. Annette felt
miserable and lost: Armand had hardly spoken to her.
Of all the bitter things she had known in her life, his
coldness and indifference were perhaps the most difficult
to bear. Then Armand stopped the cab and dragged her
into the street. They were in the dark, ugly quarter of the
Campo and the moonlight played over the damp cracked
walls and lost its last gleam in the dark doorways. It
was late and the narrow streets were empty. The few
late passers-by looked with astonishment at the elegant
young woman being dragged along by a bareheaded
young man in black clothes, who looked like a demented
priest. Then suddenly Armand stopped. An old beggar
woman was sitting on the pavement, leaning against
the wall, and as they come closer, she reached out her
hand hopefully. Without a word, Armand tore off
Annette's earrings, the necklace, the bracelets, and the
rings. Then he bent over the old woman sitting there

145

in the patch of moonlight and fastened the earrings in
her ears, clasped the necklace around her withered old
neck, and forced the rings and the bracelets on her
clawlike hands.

"Take them and keep them!" he exclaimed, between
his teeth. "They were stolen from the people and to
the people they return! They are yours."

The old hands fell heavily on the woman's lap under
the weight of emeralds and gold. She sat there staring
at Armand, her eyes wide and her mouth gaping.

Something in the woman's attitude suddenly struck
Annette. She stepped forward and leaned over her. The
mouth was still gaping and the eyes wide open. But the
old beggar woman had died of shock. Annette screamed
and turned away and began to run, sobbing with terror
and horror.

The next day the newspapers were full of what they
described as the most extraordinary mystery of the
century: the discovery, in the poorest quarter of the city,
of an old woman, a beggar, found dead, with a priceless necklace around her throat, diamond earrings in
her ears, a golden scarab pinned to her rags, and her
wrists rigid and cold in bracelets of emeralds.

Annette spent a sleepless night, pacing her bedroom
and smoking one cigarette after another. For the first

time since she had met Armand she was scared of him.
She also felt scorned and rejected, and her resentment
and fury against "the cause" was as implacable as if
Armand had preferred another woman to her. Everything that was violent, untamed, primitive in her nature
was pushing her across that narrow, slender bridge between love and hate; she was discovering in herself a
new cruelty, an imperious urge to punish, to hurt, even
to destroy. She was indulging in a turmoil of passions
and emotions such as those which had, in France, led
to so many *"crimes passionnels,"* those crimes of love
that are always forgiven by the court, and to this day
generally end in an acquittal. The next morning she took
the train to Como and sought refuge and consolation
with the only man who understood her completely.

"I cannot stand it any more, Dicky. I cannot, I cannot, I cannot! It's quite hopeless; he will drag me with
him, into the gutter or in jail. Can you see me in a jail,
Dicky?"

Glendale held her head paternally against his shoulder, trying to disguise his feeling of triumph—he felt
as if he were at last succeeding in stealing the *Giaconda*
from the Louvre.

"Please help me, Dicky! Please!"

"But, my dear, it is all so very easy! Stop seeing him.

To make it easier for you, we could go to Turkey or to Japan."

"But I can't go away, Dicky. I can't exist without him. I will always rush back to him, as long as I shall live. I love him so. My God, Dicky, what am I to do?"

"Well, I suppose there is really only one thing we can do," Glendale said slowly. "We must arrange it in such a way that you simply *couldn't* see him. It will be most painful at first, but after a year or two, life being what it is, I dare say you will be able to overcome your . . . weakness."

"It's no use running away to Turkey or to Japan. It's not far enough. I know myself."

"Then, the only thing left for us is to put you behind solid, thick walls under very strict guard, and behind iron bars, so that Armand would be out of reach completely."

"What do you mean? I can't live in a fortress."

"No, no, my dear. Not *you*. But we could have Armand locked up in one of those good old-fashioned jails that the Italians have inherited from the Austrians and have preserved so well."

She stamped her foot in anger. "Dicky, you couldn't —I forbid you. I would never see or talk to you again."

"Think it over, Annette. My health is not very good

—my doctors suspect me of getting old—a very demo-
cratic process. I have no children left. When I think of
all my houses, gardens, flowers, all my collections, left
without the loving care they have been used to . . . You
and I, we both love *things*, so you know what I mean.
They need someone to understand and to appreciate
them, to look at them lovingly, to play with them, and
pet them . . . I want you to marry me, Annette."

She stared at him incredulously. "Dicky! You don't
even know who I am."

"I know everything. I have been looking into your
past for almost a year now and there is little I haven't
found out. I can tell you more: there is no trace of your
past left anywhere. It gave me a lot of trouble, but
whoever will look for your birth certificate at the Mairie
will never find a trace of Annette Boudin there. As for
those other things which we call conventions—birth,
nobility—I don't care a damn about them—not a damn.
My wife was a gypsy and she had true nobility. The
only thing that matters in a human being is *quality*,
and that you have. You will be the perfect wife for me
and the best heir to everything I possess. Without you
my houses will sink into plushy ugliness, my paintings
will mean merely money, my gardens will be abandoned

to the indifference of retainers. . . . We cannot do that to our *things*, can we, Annette? They need us."

She smiled, in spite of herself.

"I couldn't care less about your past and I am completely sure about your future. I am, after all, a connoisseur of quality. Ask any art dealer in the world."

She was overwhelmed; she could not think of a greater tribute, of a more moving homage. But she shook her head.

"I wish I could say 'yes,' Dicky. But it's in my blood. I cannot be without Armand. You know how it is."

He nodded sadly. "Yes, my pet, I know. Well, let's not talk about it. Time will tell. Let's go to Ravenna. . . ."

He had shown her a possible escape and all night she lay with her eyes wide open, wishing she might break free. But one should not attempt the impossible— it was an old French popular saying, and she knew it well. For the first time she realized that love was perhaps the greatest of all servitudes, and that to break free one had to become a terrorist oneself and fight against its tyranny. During her next meeting with Armand she looked at him with a new attention, almost with coldness. She was trying to steel herself. They never knew where they would meet next. A brief note would summon her suddenly to a boat on the lake, where Armand would wait for her in the red shirt and blue trousers of a Como *pescatore;* and she would be lying in the fisherman's net like a captive Ondine. Then there would be a week or two of silence and a new note and she would take the train to Genoa and meet him among the plaster saints and stone figures of the Campo Santo, where he would suddenly appear between two marble statues like one more angel. They also met several times in the house of the poet Gabriele d'Annunzio, whose youthful fame was then beginning its thunderous ascent in the Italian sky. Their encounter was accidental and was typical of the d'Annunzio of the early days. They had been walking through the Campo Santo one afternoon when they noticed that a small, elegantly dressed man appeared to be following them among the statues. Thinking of the police, Armand had instantly put his hand to the pistol he carried under his arm. The young man stepped forward and took off his hat with a great display of humility—and not a little insolence.

"My name is Gabriele d'Annunzio," he said. "I am a poet. I have a most urgent request to present to you, Monsieur. Would you accept to consecrate my house?"

"I am afraid, Monsieur, I don't see what you mean."

"Would you accept to spend a night in my house so

that love and beauty would bless it forever? I hope you will not misunderstand the humble request of a poet."

D'Annunzio told this story differently. In his version, he had offered his house to a couple of young and poor lovers whom he had found kissing in the Campo Santo of Genoa, and it had very much amused Lady L. to read later that she was a young flower girl who still carried in her arms a large basket of Parma violets and who had the "incomparable beauty of an untamed animal." But one had to allow for poetic license, and she didn't mind at all being called an "untamed animal."

Then, in quick succession, two things happened which confronted Annette with the most cruel decision of her life.

One day, in answer to an urgent call from Glendale's secretary, she drove to his house and was taken immediately to his bedroom. Dicky's face was gray and his eyes sunken as he lay there, his hand was still holding a box of miniatures and he was looking at them with obvious pleasure: they had been painted by Holbein. Two men stood by his bedside, the famous heart specialist, Cassini, and Signor Felicci, an antiquarian from Milan. When the two visitors left, Glendale looked sadly at the most beautiful thing of them all, but it was a living thing, and thus it had a will and a mind of its own and was therefore the most difficult to acquire.

"Cassini gives me a year. I expect he is wrong, but that might mean as well two years as six months. My nephews must have their tongues hanging out in happy anticipation. Will you marry me?"

"But I can't, I can't, I can't!" she cried out. "I cannot live without him."

"Annette, freedom is the most precious thing on earth, as all the revolutionaries and all the philosophers have taught us. You cannot remain a slave to love for the rest of your life. You should have profited by Armand's teachings by now! You must revolt against the tyrant. You must throw a bomb at your ruthless master. Think it over, my dear, and give me your answer."

She cried silently, trying to make up her mind. She knew that this was her last chance and that there would never be another man like Dicky, but she could only shake her head with the terrible feeling that she saw a way of escape but that she did not have the strength to achieve it.

A few days later fate forced its decision upon her: she found herself pregnant. Lady L. often wondered what her life would have been if that hadn't happened: she wouldn't have been painted by Boldini and Sargent, her son wouldn't have become a duke, and her grandsons the pillars of the Tory party, and England would have lost one of her *grandes dames*. As soon as her condition became clear to her, she acted with an almost steely resolution, silencing her heart, and it was typical of her new determination that in spite of all her confidence in Dicky, she didn't reveal her pregnancy to him. She was taking no chances, fighting ruthlessly for the future of her child, with all the singlemindedness and instinct of animals who obey the oldest law of nature.

Her last meeting with Armand took place on the Borromean Islands, on Lago Maggiore. The islands were then still privately owned and she was staying there as a guest of Princess Borriglia. Armand had rowed out to meet her in a fisherman's boat on choppy water. Annette in a white dress, a white umbrella in her hand, was waiting on the marble steps leading from the landing into the Italian garden. He had followed her into the wilderness of rose bushes along the silent shore—those were the last autumnal flowers, with their heavy fragrance, the mature fragrance that comes to roses in September as deeper thoughts come to aging men.

She told him that Glendale was planning to close his house in October, putting his collections away, and that if they were to lay their hands on them, next Saturday would be the last moment to do it. She would be spending the weekend at the villa and so she would contrive to put a sleeping powder into the night watchman's wine. She would also administer it to the rest of the household, herself included, so that no one could suspect her. To this day, Lady L. remembered the almost physical pain that seemed to tear her whole body apart as she spoke; she remembered the drone of the wasps around the roses; her feeling of utter, total despair, of pity, tenderness, and her cold, cruel, bitter anger, too. To make things worse, Armand had shown himself so grateful and so pleased, his face shone with such an expression of delight, and he looked so beautiful and young and full of hope that she couldn't bear it any longer, and threw herself into his arms and sobbed helplessly against his shoulder. She had almost confessed everything; but fortunately the young anarchist, before she had time to speak, lunged into a fiery tirade, describing the way ahead with such realism that she knew once more that it had to be, that there was no other way.

"I must tell you that something has happened that will be of historical importance to the movement," he told her excitedly. "A new explosive has been discovered. It is easy to make and it is a hundred times more powerful than anything we have yet known."

"How wonderful," she said.

"We shall be able to achieve truly great things. It will take only a few determined men to blow up the strongest bastions of authority. The discovery of formula 5.A.100 by the American scientists opens a new and bright road for humanity . . ."

"I'm sure it does," she told him.

There was nothing left for her now but irony. It was at that precise moment, as, the tears trembling on her cheeks, she was looking at a rose and a wasp dancing around it, that the caustic, sophisticated and sometimes ruthless Lady L. was truly born. For the rest of her life she was to appear to the world as a little unkind; and her lightning-quick, whimsical and sometimes lashing wit, her *bons mots* made her both admired and feared, while the most thoughtful among her friends often were left wondering what secret wound had sharpened those claws.

She drew back, looked at his inspired face once more, and sighed profoundly: God shouldn't make his enemies so beautiful, she thought, it is so wrong. It seemed to her that this lovely, pale, forlorn face of a true poet was already staring at her from behind the prison's bars. Such an injustice! It was so cruel of him to treat her so, to force her to do such a terrible thing to him—she would never forgive him—never, as long as she lived.

"Please don't cry," he begged her tenderly. "It will work out all right. It's a good plan and it cannot fail."

How was it possible, she asked herself, that for so many years he had been able to outwit all the police of Europe—that he had never been caught? Oh well, she thought, the police is run by men, not by women, that's why, I suppose.

The wasp was still dancing around the rose.

It was agreed that Armand and his two friends would arrive at Como on Friday night; that they would enter the villa of Count Granowski, which had stood shut and abandoned for several months after the owner's bankruptcy; that, on Saturday afternoon, Annette would take a walk past the villa and throw a red rose on the path behind the main gate, as a sign that everything was well and that there had been no change in plans. Then at ten o'clock they would enter the house and, filling their bags, they would return to the Granowski villa, change to uniforms of Austrian and French cavalry officers— the annual *Concours Hippique* was then taking place in Como—and proceed to Genoa by the night train. From there they would take the steamer to Constantinople, which was at that time the greatest free market for stolen goods in the world, beyond the reach of European police. The name Constantinople filled Annette with such romantic longing that once more she almost had a change of heart—she could see herself in a gilded caïque on the Bosporus, in the arms of her lover.

Since then, Lady L. had been several times to Istanbul, as it was now called, and she had always loved it, but naturally it was not at all the same thing without Armand. Oh, well, she thought, I suppose one cannot have everything in life.

The red rose was duly found by Armand lying on the path on the agreed afternoon. He picked it up and was a little surprised to see that it was not a fresh flower but that it was made of tulle. Annette had torn it from one of her hats. She had decided against a living rose because it lasts so briefly; and she wanted Armand to keep something that would make him always remember her.

The three men met with no difficulties when they entered the villa. The door had been left open; the servants had been drugged and so had the guests, among them the British Consul in Milan, the German General von Ludekindt, captain of his country's cavalry team to the *Concours Hippique,* and two or three others whose names and faces Lady L. had long forgotten. Dicky had merely pretended to be drugged; he had to be careful, with his heart. Annette had given herself a more than generous dose: she knew that otherwise she wouldn't have slept a wink that night. After a quick three quarters of an hour's work, Armand, Lecoeur and the jockey had returned to the Granowski villa with their loot. They had hardly entered the garden when twenty men set upon them from all sides; Armand and the jockey were overpowered at once, but Lecoeur, with a horrible oath, had still managed to pull his old apache knife and stab one of the policemen in the chest. They were taken to Milan, and for several days the arrest of Armand Denis and his band filled the European newspapers and made the *bourgeoisie* breathe easier, until the exploits of his most famous French disciple, Ravachol, reminded them that the days of the revolutionaries were far from over.

Lady L. rested her head against the cherry tree behind the wooden bench. Her eyes were closed and she was smiling. The Poet Laureate looked frightened.

They were in sight of the pavilion now, on the narrow path between the branches of lilac. There were little statues of cupids with their bows and arrows, half hidden under the wild rose bushes, and the air nearby was so thick with fragrance that all in all Sir Percy felt that at the age of eighty Lady L. shouldn't be following this path.

159

He still tried desperately to believe that the tale was a pure invention, but as it progressed, he felt more and more convinced that it had an awful, unmistakable ring of truth about it. He had known Glendale well. The Duke had always been a perfect nuisance to the Crown, the most unpredictable eccentric, with a truly anarchistic streak in his nature. He had once gone so far as to offer to the Prince of Wales a gold cigar-cutter made like a miniature guillotine. He wondered once more what it was that Lady L. had hidden in the summer pavilion—whatever it was, he didn't care for it and he didn't want to see it. If only one tenth of her story was true, it was bound to be something ghastly. Looking toward the end of the path, he could see the little latticed wooden wall, like a discreet screen which sheltered the entrance to the pavilion, thickly covered with climbing roses and trails of ivy; and the whole secretive atmosphere of a lovers' hideaway made him feel self-conscious and even a little frightened.

"My marriage was a brilliant affair," Lady L. said. "We went to live in England, where my son was born. Dicky lived longer than his doctors had expected and everybody thought I had something to do with it. The English aristocrats raised their brows at first, but then my genealogy was excellent and the portraits of my noble ancestors, whom Dicky and I chose with loving

care at Venetian antiquarians' shops and Florentine junk
shops, had been properly restored and looked very convincing—and so the criticism died down sooner than we
had expected. The Prince of Wales let it be known that I
was charming, and although until the death of Queen
Victoria I had never been received at Court, it was much
more because of her ancient feud with Dicky than because of our marriage. I took my duties very seriously.
I soon knew *Burke's Peerage* by heart and never made a
single mistake. As mistress of Glendale House I had
sixty servants—grooms, gardeners, maids—and when
we moved for the winter season to our London house
there was no end to the balls, parties, and invitations. I
never suffered from the slightest remorse, and when I
held my little boy in my arms I knew that I had done the
right thing. I did my best to forget, my very best. I
fought bravely. I gave the best parties, the most brilliant
dinners, and the most cultivated people of Europe were
constantly my guests. I became one of the most famous
and sought-after women of my time. At my table affairs
of state were discussed and my advice was eagerly
sought. When Dicky died, three years later, I did as
he had wished, and my houses, my gardens remain to
this day the most beautiful in Europe. I married Lord
L.—good servants were already difficult to come by—

161

and helped him, as you well know, with his political career. I learned a lot. I spent my nights reading, and books became my best and only trusted friends. Painters, writers, musicians surrounded me and when I showed some eccentricity of taste, it merely set a new standard. My son was a lovely boy, with dark, burning eyes, and he must have often wondered why, after staring at him, his mother would suddenly begin to cry. I had done my best to forget—concerts, races, plays, books, conversation— I had tried everything. But my shoulders were still the coldest, the loneliest things in the world. For almost eight years I had been locked behind thick walls and fought my gay and losing battle. Then, one night. . ."

CHAPTER TEN

The window was open. Night lay still and deep behind the gardens, and if there were any stars, the eye couldn't reach them. Lady L. was sitting in a red Venetian chair, her eyes closed, listening to the distant sound of Scarlatti barely audible through the closed doors. She had left the concert room and her guests to have a glass of wine and smoke a cigarette. She loved to be alone—almost as much as she hated to be lonely. She had asked the Szilagi Quartet to give a concert at the house, but in the last year or two, something had happened to music. It had become almost too painful, too evocative of happiness. The cigarette was burning out between her long fingers.

There was a discreet cough and she opened her eyes. She was still alone in the room. Then, under the thick red curtain she caught sight of a black boot. She stared at it—without fear, for she had been too intimate with fear and it took more than the sight of a black boot under a curtain to make her feel scared. Even when the curtain was moved aside and a man stepped forward and faced her, she felt nothing but a slight curiosity and a tinge of annoyance. He was a heavy man, with short arms, white stubby hands, shabby clothes and a black bowler hat on his head. What struck her most were his feet— they were enormous and the boots looked particularly clumsy and ugly and were covered with mud. The second thing she noticed was that he hadn't removed his hat. He stood there, with the black bowler sitting far back on his head, and stared at her fixedly, with a strange, almost avid curiosity and an uncertain smile that hesitated between impudence and obsequiousness.

"Plato—Plato is the name," the man suddenly said in a hoarse voice. "Always ready to serve—always will-

ing, always happy to oblige. Great friend of freedom—
determined to make the prison walls crumble everywhere. Spent some time in prison myself—for strictly
humanitarian motives—hated every moment of it, had
to quit. Died several times on the barricades—rein-
carnated again—obviously deemed indispensable to the
world. A glass of wine would be appreciated."

Lady L. watched him coldly with a sort of detached,
scientific interest, as if he were an insect or a toad. In a
way she was almost enjoying herself: it was a relief
after all those years to meet somebody at last whom she
really *knew*—although she had never seen him before.
The man took a step forward, his little blue eyes jerking
constantly around the room. She could clearly see that
he was scared and unsure of himself. There was something both repulsive and helpless in his small features,
pinkish nose, cherubic lips, and in the round, babyish,
nervous face under the black bowler that was a little
too small for him.

"A very personal matter—discretion assured—a message of importance—had a bad time getting here—dogs
barking—a very dark night—but got here—there is
nothing Plato wouldn't do for a friend—and for freedom."

His tiny, alcoholic eyes were fixed now on the bottle

of wine, and he smacked his lips quite audibly. Lady L. knew that a guest or a servant could come in at any moment and that it wouldn't do at all to be caught enjoying such company. For she did enjoy it. It was, literally, like a breath of fresh air to her. After all those years of polite society, of protocol, of propriety, of good manners and convention, of hours spent thinking who should sit next to whom at the table, the vulgarity of the man, his impudence, his heavy, muddy boots on the carpet and the hat that he disrespectfully kept on his head, were a welcome contrast. For one brief moment and for the first time in a long while, she suddenly thought of her father. But she couldn't afford such self-indulgence. Her son was asleep in his room and she simply couldn't be caught smiling pleasantly to this unpalatable character as if to a long-lost friend. She frowned and raised her hand to the bell rope. Then, with an extraordinary quickness, quite unexpected from him, the man removed his bowler hat and, as if he were performing a conjurer's trick, he produced from it a red tulle rose and held it raised in his hand in mid-air.

There was still an uncertainty on his face and Annette knew instantly that he didn't know what the red tulle rose meant, why he had been asked to enter one of the

greatest houses of England and present it to the famous
Lady L.

She stared silently at the rose. She did not gasp, she
did not move. There was no expression on her face. She
knew how not to give herself away: after all, she was a
skilled professional herself. The man waited almost pathetically, rose in hand, and as she still showed no trace
of fear or even of understanding, he began to shrink,
his cheeks began to tremble, drops of sweat appeared on
his forehead—he pressed his bowler hat against his chest
and his blue eyes darted toward the open window.

"Obviously a mistake—a regrettable error— Her
Ladyship will excuse—an old friend of nobility, a most
humble servant of the crown—a message delivered to
the wrong door—a dirty trick played on poor Plato by
some French ex-jailbird whom he had helped in the good-
ness of his heart . . ."

He began to back away toward the window. Lady L.
was still looking at the rose. It hadn't aged a bit. Just as
she thought.

"What was the message?" she asked curtly. "You had
better tell me everything or I will have you flogged so
that you will regret the day you were born. What was
the message?"

The man still looked uncertain and bewildered, but

there was now a trace of hope in his watery eyes and the beginning of a smile on his lips.

"An unfinished business—something that happened in Como many years ago—a certain plan that had gone wrong—but that can still be carried out . . ."

A friend of his, who should be nameless, a very noble young man—who had been kept eight years behind the walls of an Italian prison—all a simple misunderstanding—had managed to escape—after several attempts, and had now reached England—help was bitterly needed —police everywhere—had asked Plato to deliver this message—a certain promise had apparently been made —and had to be kept.

"How is he?" Lady L. asked.

"Oh, all right, perfectly all right, but in great danger —lying low at a certain place . . ."

He was watching her carefully. Although she didn't say much, he was obviously beginning to feel at ease. He extended his hand, took hold of the wine bottle and, taking Lady L.'s glass, filled it and brought it to his lips. It was evident from his behavior that he no longer felt himself in danger, and as Lady L. did not move or protest he proceeded to fill his glass again. But the fact was that Lady L. had forgotten about him. Her heart was beating fast and violently, but it had nothing to do with

fear. Her whole body seemed suddenly to have abandoned her—it was more than a weakness but like some
sort of total emptiness, as if her blood had gone away
and as if her whole body cried for it to return. The
words of her old friend Oscar Wilde rang in her ears:
"I can resist anything except temptation," and she
smiled. She placed her hand against her heart—a gesture that her attentive visitor once more mistakenly
attributed to fear.

It was thought that Her Ladyship would perhaps
kindly arrange for a fancy-dress ball at her house—
something very elegant—to give the charming ladies the
opportunity to wear their jewels—that was very important—an enchanting evening—plenty of music—something truly light and gay. The two gentlemen who were
in such dire predicament could then safely join the
masquerade in disguise and, when the last waltz was
over—the company could perhaps board a steamer—
taking a few things with them—and sail on a pleasure
cruise to Turkey—the Golden Horn—the Bosporus, the
minarets—very romantic—apparently it was all agreed
years ago.

Lady L. knew that those were Armand's words and
that there was nothing else to do but to obey. He had her
at his mercy entirely; and if she didn't really care if she

had to fall from her pedestal, the future of her son was at stake, and this was another matter. So she had no choice left but to obey. But to her own surprise, the fact that she had no choice and that she couldn't do anything else was almost a relief. She only wished that Dicky were alive to help her. She could almost hear his cold, ironic tone: "Well, my dear, considering that there is nothing else you can do, why not have some fun doing it?"

She considered the plan calmly and coldly. Professionally speaking, it was quite good. There was little doubt that her fashionable friends would come wearing their best jewels—they always did—and, changing into their fancy dress, most of them would leave the jewels in their rooms.

The sounds of Scarlatti were still coming from the concert hall. Plato had now had several glasses of wine and, the alcohol adding to the nervous reaction after his alarm, he was getting perceptibly drunk. His watery eyes observed Lady L. attentively. Then the music stopped suddenly, and a burst of applause was heard from the house. Lady L. got up. Plato tittered and lifted a finger.

Of course, things could be arranged—he was always willing to help a lady in distress. The two men were hidden, as he had said, at a certain place. Now, if the gracious lady only showed herself understanding and would sign certain papers that would guarantee poor Plato, let us say, a thousand a year—the police could make a certain discovery—or perhaps, should we say, two thousand pounds.

He suddenly dared to extend his hand and put his arm around Lady L.'s waist. She hit him quick and hard, and he doubled up in pain and surprise, looking at her incredulously, his face collapsing into frightened pitifulness.

"Did you say there were two of them?"

"Two, Your Ladyship," Plato said, cringing. "A handsome Frenchman and a sad little Irish fellow with a broken neck. There were three of them, but one got himself killed during the escape."

"All right, then," Lady L. said. "I will give a ball on the second weekend of May. Come and see me next week again. We'll fix the details. And remember, if something happens to my friends—they are my friends, you understand—something will happen to Plato—he will be a dead duck."

He looked at her imploringly. It was obvious that it was all too much for him—he was both scared and amazed—that the only dangerous thing about him was his weakness.

"What about a little money?"

She took off a ring from her finger and gave it to him. "Sell it. Now go."

He gave her another injured and reproachful look, put his bowler hat back on his head and walked to the French window. She noticed that he had flat feet, and almost laughed. He stopped again, looked back, and said with immense self-pity, in a high nasal tone, "Poor Plato, never through the door, always through the window, and always back into the night."

Then he was gone.

Lady L. sank back into her chair and remained motionless. The music had begun again and the sounds of a Schumann concerto were coming from the distance. Her heart kept beating wildly and she remained there smiling, almost triumphant, looking at the red tulle rose that she held in her hand.

CHAPTER ELEVEN

The Poet Laureate sat stiffly in a low Victorian chair: the gros-point embroidery represented lapdogs, lions, and deer, all crowded sweetly together in the Garden of Eden. Sir Percy had never been inside the summer pavilion before, and he looked around him warily, with a strong trace of disapproval and even of suspicion. After all that Lady L. had already told him, it was clear that some dastardly things must have happened here. There was something indecent about the place, anyway. There was, for instance, a large—much too large—bed, an unpleasant, gilded affair, obviously Oriental, with a canopy and a clouded mirror over it. He didn't care for it at all. The whole damned place had a strong Oriental atmosphere. There were strange Persian portraits on the walls—stiff, bearded figures glancing sidelong under pointed fur caps. There were Turkish lanterns, Russian icons, far too many cushions, and a screen with a collection of various Queens of Spades plastered all over it. Against the wall a Madras strongbox, studded with silver nails and brass plates, looked like a gigantic castle from some monstrous game of chess. There were portraits of Lady L.'s deceased pets everywhere: some of them were painted in over the human faces of Lord L.'s family portraits. Dogs, cats, monkeys, parrots, hedgehogs and budgereegahs, some of them in eighteenth-century noblemen's costume, looked proudly at Sir Percy Rodiner from their gilded frames. It had always been her favorite hobby: he had seen her spend hours, with tears in her eyes, painting in the likeness of some newly deceased pet over the face of one of Lord L.'s most distinguished ancestors. Cats in armor, cats standing proudly on the bridge of a flagship in admiral's attire and watching the enemy through telescopes, cats on horseback in the uniform of the Bengal Lancers, dogs in scarlet Guards' uniforms clutching proudly a parchment with the family motto, *Tenir*, written on it, parrots who had taken over the pose of some long-departed grandmother, kittens' faces imposed on a group of stiffly posed children, and one particularly dashing black cat on horseback pointing his sword at the enemy, his tail clasping a lance with fluttering pennon.

"That's darling Timmy," Lady L. said, catching Sir Percy's glance. "He's leading the Charge of the Light Brigade."

Sir Percy gave her a disapproving look. Lady L. was seated in the other chair sipping a sherry. She looked a little upset, as she always did when talking about some of her departed pets. The Poet Laureate stirred uneasily. There was something in the atmosphere of the place that filled him with apprehension and made him very nervous. The air was stuffy, stale—without the feeling of living things outside. The Moorish shutters were closed, and whatever light there was squeezed in almost cringingly and lay weakly on the Caucasian carpets, among the cushions and Turkish narghiles. It occurred suddenly to Sir Percy that perhaps her anarchist friends of sixty years ago had used the pavilion to hide their stock of bombs there. The bombs could have been hidden anywhere, in the Zanzibar chest studded with ivory and mother-of-pearl, under the bed, or in the massive strongbox where the Indian bankers used to keep their gold and which Glendale had brought back with him from his travels.

"Well, what happened then?" he asked gruffly.

He was beginning to believe her story: there was something about the place that somehow made it sound true. He glanced at the bed again: a disgusting affair that occupied too much place and simply didn't look right in England.

"That's a Tunisian bed," Lady L. said, catching his eye again. "I bought it myself in Kairouan. It comes directly from the Beylical harem."

"What did you do then?" Sir Percy insisted disapprovingly.

"Two weeks to give a truly successful fancy ball is very little time, so I was kept awfully busy. And to make things worse, the Prince and Princess of Wales had announced their gracious intention of visiting us during the next weekend on their way back from Bath, and that meant at least twenty guests for breakfast, lunch, tea, and dinner. I had about sixty-five servants, not counting my husband, but it was my responsibility to insure that the guests were comfortable, the rules of protocol strictly

and smoothly adhered to, the guests properly seated at
the ceremonial meals, and all the social amenities and
proprieties strictly observed. It took up a great deal of
my time and energy—but then, I was really living in a
sort of happy trance, for I knew that after the tedious and
stifling politeness of entertaining the Royalties, I should
see Armand again—and nothing else seemed to matter.
It was the most wonderful relief to know that I had no
choice, really, for I was entirely at his mercy now. The
scandal about my past would have shaken England and
destroyed my son's future, and so I was spared any
moral dilemmas or soul-searching anxieties. There was
nothing I could do about it except make the best of it,
which I was determined to do. And so I went about my
duties with a light heart—working out the rules of
protocol for the princely visit, planning my table so as to
give each noble guest the status due him. My husband
still nursed the hope of getting himself appointed as
British Ambassador to France, you know, and naturally
the Prince of Wales could be of invaluable help to him
—so I was determined to do my best. I must say it did
occur to me that it might be fun to be the British
Ambassadress in Paris—seeing the city from such a
different angle, so to speak—but it all depended on my
meeting with Armand, of course, and on how much he

really loved me and cared about me; but perhaps, somehow, the two things could be reconciled—particularly
in Paris, where it is always easier to attend to matters
of the heart. The most important thing of all, practically
speaking, was that the fancy ball and the jewel robbery
go off without a hitch, so that it didn't leave a stain on
my reputation. I spent hours writing out the invitations
for the ball, trying to remember everyone to whom I had
to be civil, so as not to make anyone feel slighted, and
I have to admit that I enjoyed putting down the names of
some of my more arrogant friends, whom I simply
longed to see part with their ostentatious jewels. I had
the feeling that somehow Dicky was guiding my hand,
and I could almost hear his voice saying, 'Darling, you
simply *must* invite the Marchioness of Terrence; she
oughtn't to go on wearing that hideous tiara!'

"It was all rather fun. But there were also moments of
apprehension and even of panic. What would Armand's
attitude be? Did he suspect the part I had played in his
arrest in Como? It didn't matter, though: we loved each
other much too much to mind the cruelty or the pain
we had caused each other. It would all be forgotten in
the first kiss. But then a deeper anxiety would clutch at
my heart, and leaving my pencil and my list, I would
rush to the eastern wing of the house, where the nursery

was, grab my son in my arms, and bury my face in his dark curls; whatever was to happen to his mother during the fateful meeting, he was not in danger; no one knew, his future was secure, the game was won. He was only seven years old and still gay as a kitten, and my happiness was such that I wished I could share it with him. I wished I could tell him everything and I knew that if only he were a little older he could have approved and forgiven.

"Plato came once more to see me, very properly this time, through the main entrance, in broad daylight. He listened to me very sheepishly, his bowler hat in hand, his knees shaking under him and throwing disbelieving, almost superstitiously scared glances toward the Prince of Wales, who was walking with my husband on the lawn. As he stood there on his enormous, spread feet, bowing constantly, I suddenly thought that with a little training he would perhaps make a good butler, although I did remember that he drank too much."

CHAPTER TWELVE

The guests had begun to arrive in the afternoon, coming by train, and were met at the station by carriages. Those who came earlier were received in the Italian garden, where tea had been laid out under a splendid tent; it was a superb Italian affair which had belonged to the King of Naples and was richly decorated with the most frivolous angels, pink-bottomed cupids, cherubs blowing their trumpets, and winged chariots flying across blue skies.

The guests changed into their costumes in their rooms, and a string of giggling servants soon began bustling along the corridors carrying turbans, powdered wigs, and false beards, while shrieks for a lost black patch for a pirate's eye, or a misplaced musketeer's lace collar, issued from behind the bedroom doors. There were more than fifty guests staying in the house, and a great many had brought their servants with them, who had to be put up, too; some had even summoned their hairdressers and tailors for a final touch of perfection.

Lady L. was dressed as the Duchess of Alba, whose portrait by Goya hung in the Pink Drawing Room; and before joining her guests downstairs, she stood wearing her black mantilla and with the red tulle rose in her hair before her exact replica in the golden frame, looking in silent supplication at the divine Duchess who had loved so much and so well. Lord L., after much hesitation, had chosen the costume of a Venetian doge and she couldn't repress a smile remembering that the Venetian doges were officially and solemnly married to the deep sea.

The buffet was already crowded at ten o'clock while the first orchestra was playing the romantic Hungarian nonsense Lady L. always liked with her meals. A little after nine, while the waltz was already sending its first whirl of dancers onto the floor, Lady L. ran down the steps of the eastern entrance and out into the park. Moonlight glittered on the leaves of the trees and it looked as if millions of silver fish were swimming and pulsating in the dark waters of the night, and the brightly lit windows of the house gave to the shadows a depth and opacity that no star could pierce.

Lady L. walked quickly along the path to the summer pavilion. Music followed her; her whole body was filled with a pulsating weakness; tides of panic, delight, hope, fear, and excitement played with her heart; her smile was provoking, but a little guilty, and arrogant, too, for she suddenly knew that she *was* the Duchess of Alba and that her unhappy Goya was waiting for her. Through the door of the summer pavilion a narrow beam of light fell at her feet. She walked in.

The jockey was standing to the left of the chimney in orange and black silks: her husband's racing colors. She had simply taken the silks from the stables and had left them on the bed. Armand stood to the right, in the gray costume of the eighteenth-century French marquis that she had prepared for him. The clothes suited him perfectly for size: she had remembered his body well.

She walked in with a smile but now she stood there in tears, pressing her hand against her heart, feeling lightheaded, and blinded. She waited for him to strike her, perhaps to kill her, but not before he had taken her into his arms once more.

"Oh, my darling," she cried, "why have you done this to me?"

She felt his lips against hers and then his voice, the voice that had such strange power over her that she could never quite hear the words.

"I didn't enjoy those eight years, myself. Something went wrong—the police were waiting for us—"

He didn't know. He didn't even suspect her. But of course he didn't, he was such a naïve soul. . . . Again the old, almost maternal desire to protect him filled her with warmth; with all his cleverness, he was so innocent, so helpless! He was the sort of man who couldn't do without a woman to take care of him. She took his face between her hands and looked at him. It had barely aged, but there were touches of gray over his temples and a deeper sadness in his eyes.

"You will never know what those years without you were like," she told him, still holding his face between her hands. "I hated you for it. We could have been so happy."

She suddenly caught the eye of the jockey. The Irishman was staring at her sadly, and she felt immediately convinced that *he* knew. Or perhaps it was merely the way his broken neck made him keep his head twisted to one side, like an old disbelieving bird. There was something tragic in his narrow face. She felt embarrassed and guilty—much more guilty toward the little man than toward Armand, because she loved Armand, but Sapper had spent eight years in jail without reason. Plato was hiding discreetly behind the Madras strongbox. He was dressed as a Franciscan friar and he looked the part perfectly.

"Let's go," Armand said.

Plato offered some resistance. "I'll wait here," he suggested. "I'm frightened. Bad heart—not used to emotions—hate direct action—always at my best behind the scenes . . ."

"Come on, beauty," Armand told him. "You are not the sort of man one cares to leave behind. I don't trust you that much. Come on, pick up your feet and let's go."

From the distance, the house looked like a huge, brightly lit music box. The jockey was walking ahead of them, pushing the reluctant and muttering Plato. They followed in the shadows; she was holding his hand and pressing it with such force that she could feel her own blood pulsating in her fingers.

"Will you come with me to Turkey?" he asked.

"Please, Armand, don't ask me. I cannot do it like that. I will join you there later."

"When?"

"In a few weeks. As soon as this thing quiets down."

"I will be waiting for you."

"I will come as soon as I can. But a scandal won't help either of us. Please trust me."

In the ballroom, the waltz was in full swing. They crossed the terrace and entered through different doors: the jockey, thoughtful but unconcerned, in his black and orange silks, with the riding crop in hand; Plato sweating and trembling in his friar's robe, throwing panic-stricken glances left and right as if he were making up his mind through which window to jump out; and together, through another door, a handsome marquis was seen offering his arm to the Duchess of Alba. They were such a striking couple that, as they moved onto the dance floor and began to waltz, the pirates, the Columbines, the odalisques, the Arabian sheiks, and all the inevitable Napoleons, maharajahs, and Carmens instinctively made room for them.

"Where are the bags?"

"In my room. But please, Armand, please don't do

it. I will give you my own jewels. They are worth a fortune."

"Annette, it is a matter of principle. I want all those leeches, who live on workers like parasites, to spit out the blood they have sucked."

"Please, Armand, it's dangerous. Something might go wrong again—like in Como."

"It will be all right."

"I don't want to lose you again—please take my jewels."

"My dear Annette, but of course I will take your jewels. They also have been taken away from the people. But I will take everything away from all those parasites as well. I hate their guts. If I could hurt them more, another way, I would. But that is the only place where you can hurt them—in their money."

"Armand . . ."

"Yes."

"How am I to find you in Constantinople?"

"I will write to you as soon as I am there."

The waltz ended. It was agreed that they would meet in the billiard room, after the next dance. Then Armand, Plato, and the jockey would go through the bedrooms while the ball would be at its gayest and gather the valuables. She left him, went upstairs and into the nursery. The little boy was asleep, breathing peacefully in the moonlight. She stood over him silently, trying to think, trying to regain hold of herself, to remember who she was, where she belonged. She wasn't sure any longer. Was she Annette, the girl from the streets of Paris, ready to throw everything away for love's sake, or was she Lady L., the respected, feared, toasted Lady L.—"the woman," as one of the socialite weeklies had described her, "who had everything"? The only safe, certain thing she could cling to in her turmoil was the peaceful face of her sleeping child. She leaned over him and pressed her face against his head. He stirred, murmured, but didn't wake up. Then she left him and walked down the stairs again. She stopped once more in front of the Duchess of Alba and arranged her mantilla and the red rose in her hair. We do look alike, she thought. I wonder if you, too, wanted to have everything.

In the billiard room, a red-capped, long-tailed and horned Mephistopheles was discussing the latest news from South Africa with a John Bull in top hat and heavy boots. A black-bearded Arabian sheik with a menacing dagger in his belt, who also happened to be the Dutch Ambassador to the Court of St. James's, was giving his opinion on the Prussian situation to a fat pirate with a cutlass, his head tied in a red bandanna:

he was St. John Smith, the Permanent Secretary of the Foreign Office. Chief Justice Oliphant, one of the sternest disciplinarians of his time, who had sent more criminals behind iron bars than any other distinguished member of his profession, had come dressed as Casanova, which showed, Lady L. thought, that at least he was not beyond dreaming; in his white wig and black silk cap, he was sipping champagne and talking to a Franciscan friar who looked very nervous and whose eyes were literally running away from him; he gave Lady L. a desperate imploring glance—it was a call for help.

"Yes, Your Honor—I quite agree with you there, Your Honor," Plato was saying in a hoarse, mechanical voice, obviously not conscious of what the conversation was about. "As Disraeli said to me once—well, whatever he said to me, he was perfectly right—a great man, Disraeli—wish he were still alive—used to shoot grouse together—or was it partridge?—anyway, in season only, only in season—strictly legal—never poached in my whole life—stick to the law, before the law sticks to you, that's my rule."

He edged away, moving backward, and almost grabbed Lady L. by the arm, panting heavily. His face was sweating so profusely that the eyes themselves appeared to be swimming in some oily substance.

"This is too much—this man here—the judge—sent me to jail three years ago—asks me now if we hadn't met before—this is not for Plato—Plato has done what he was hired for—arranged it all—a man of planning, of thought, not of action—need a glass of port badly— all shaken up—poor Plato—tell them to hurry."

In the billiard room, Armand was standing in a corner surrounded by three enraptured ladies, one of them dressed as Queen Marie Antoinette, another as a fish-wife, and the third as Ophelia—or was it Juliet? She was at leasty twenty years too old for either, Lady L. thought. Armand excused himself with a bow and went over to her.

"Plato is scared stiff," Lady L. told him. "You should have picked a better man for the job. He looks like a punctured balloon. He is going to die of fright any moment."

Armand shrugged. "Well, they won't find out what scared him at the autopsy. I cannot understand how our comrades in Milan could have recommended him to me. They said that he was the last anarchist left in England. He is not a safe man to leave behind, so I had to take him along. Anyway, there weren't enough of us. I had no choice. We will begin in half an hour, when the ball is in full swing."

They went out on the terrace and stood in the moonlight with the laughter and the music and the dancing shadows behind them. Lady L. put her hand to her throat, her eyes closed, and breathed in the cool air of the night.

She remembered the old, lined, sarcastic face of the man who had given her everything—and yet had taken everything away from her.

"Take me away with you, Armand," she said, her eyes still closed. "Take me away with you."

"Not now. You will be more useful to us in your present position. You will be able to help us better."

She looked at him in disbelief.

"To *us?*" she asked. "Is there anyone else who exists except you and me?"

He kissed her hand—a marquis kissing the hand of the Duchess of Alba on the moonlit terrace.

"There are millions of us, Annette—millions—famished, enslaved, fear- and disease-stricken millions. We belong to them. You will join us in Constantinople later. We will wait for you."

An unbearable feeling of injustice filled her heart.

"Listen," she cried out, "listen to me. I will leave everything for you. I will leave my child, my position, my pleasures, my luxury, my houses, and all my lovely things—I will ruin myself for you gladly—but for you alone. Not for millions of other people, anonymous millions whose faces I don't know. I will give up everything to be with you—but you alone. I don't want to have humanity for a rival—a rival you will always prefer to me. I don't want *Liberté, Egalité,* and *Fraternité* to shadow us forever, to always grab every shred of personal happiness away from us—they look like Plato, all three of them, and I don't ever want to see ugly faces again. I will sacrifice everything to be with you—but you must sacrifice a little, too. There is not enough room in your heart for the whole of mankind and for myself as well. I want a lot of room, Armand, I want all the room, I want to be your only cause— I will gladly help you to rob all my friends, and I will leave behind me all my pleasures and content myself with happiness."

They were playing a gay, quick, feminine waltz now, and its very lightness seemed to lift all the burdens from the earth. She could clearly see his face in the moonlight, and there was infinite sadness in it.

"During all those years in prison, I longed for nothing else but you," he said. "I only wish I were free. But I am not. *I believe.* I belong to my faith. You cannot ask me to castrate myself. You don't want to hold in your

arms the shadow of a man. I have to fight on for my
beliefs, Annette. That's why nature made a man a man."

She stood there in the shadows and looked at him,
and his face was half lit from the lamps by the window
—the other half belonged to the moon. She was trying
to understand, to share, to see with his eyes—but she
could not. To love and to be loved was all that mattered
—the only reason to live, the only worthy cause; the
rest belonged to the moon. Her lips began to tremble—
she felt rejected and scorned—then, abruptly, she
stamped her foot furiously.

"I want you, I want you!" she cried out. "I want
you for myself alone and I will find a way to keep you
for myself forever!"

"Annette! Please try to understand. It's difficult to be
a man."

In his courtier's dress, he looked more aristocratic
than, and superior to, any nobleman that she had ever
known. Yes, she thought, that is what he is: an aristocrat of feeling, and a corrupted aristocrat at that, who
sacrifices everything for his self-indulgent, exquisite
thoughts. But I will find a way, she told him silently,
and you will belong to me and to no one else.

"Let's go in."

CHAPTER THIRTEEN

Sir Percy Rodiner looked around him with suspicion: he hoped that she had a really good reason for
bringing him here, for it was just not the sort of place
where he would care to be seen. There was a clock
hidden somewhere, probably behind the screen with
the Queen of Spades plastered all over it, and its
regular, implacable ticking sounded particularly omi-
nous; after all this talk about bombs, it made one feel

as if a time mechanism had been set in motion, perhaps even sixty years ago, and that the entire grisly place, with all its romantic rubbish, would be suddenly blown up in a thousand pieces. The whole atmosphere of the pavilion had something disreputable about it; it was strangely evocative and suggestive and one couldn't avoid certain thoughts here. . . . There were, for instance, pseudo-Oriental pictures on the walls—turbaned ladies swooning in the arms of exotic lovers, beside the Bosporus; lithographs of the seraglio; two or three Delacroix sketches of romantic, dashing Arab horsemen with a not very resistant captive thrown across the saddle; lovers everywhere, embracing in troikas, in the snow, under palm trees, kissing on the usual balconies under the usual moonlight. It was all worthless stuff; the only objects of any value were the two Tiepolos representing harem scenes. The Poet Laureate had not known that Tiepolo had painted the Orient, too. Italy was bad enough.

"I didn't know you cared for such romantic nonsense," Sir Percy said.

Lady L. was leaning back in her chair, playing with her gay Indian shawl. She was staring at something lovingly and Sir Percy quickly followed her glance, only to be confronted by the face of a deceased pet: a

196

huge tabby cat in a French sailor's suit. He wondered irritably over whose face she would paint his own like-ness when he joined the ranks of her departed pets.

"There are a lot of things here that I couldn't put any-where else," Lady L. said slowly. "This is the sort of house I could have had in Constantinople, over the Golden Horn, and the sort of objects I would then have had around me. Some of them have a great sentimental value to me."

She shook her head—a sharp, quick, provocative movement with a touch of defiance in it.

"I have spent a great deal of my life in this place, regretting what might have been, but comforted by my things," she said.

It is strange, she thought, how quickly sixty years can pass and how little one forgets. She could almost hear the music of the ball and see the couples on the floor, the orchestra in their Austrian gold-laced uniforms, the jockey standing in the Renaissance Room in his black and orange silks, holding his riding crop and talking to a group of men who were staring at him with very serious attention—they all had been drinking. One of them was Sir John Evatt, whose horse, Zephyr, had won the Derby that year.

"You mean to say you rode Hurricane in its last race?" Evatt was saying.

"I did, sir," the jockey answered, a little belligerently.

"And you mean to say that you rode Syrius for the Rothschilds?"

"I did, sir," Sapper answered. "A mighty fine horse Syrius was, sir."

"And that you have won the Grand National twice?"

"I did, sir," Sapper said. "I did indeed, sir."

The three men looked at him frigidly.

"Then I can tell that you came here dressed up as 'Sapper' O'Malley, the famous little Irish jockey who broke his neck ten years ago in Paris at the Grand Prix du Bois."

"I did indeed, sir," Sapper said.

"A mighty great jockey, Sapper was," Evatt said.

"I share your opinion there, sir," Sapper said.

"Great pity he broke his neck," Evatt said.

"Great pity—great pity indeed, sir."

"Wonder what's happened to him?" Evatt asked.

"Quite a lot, sir, quite a lot."

"He was the greatest of them all," Evatt said.

"So he was, sir," Sapper said.

"There will never be another like him again," Evatt said.

"He was truly the one and only of his kind, sir," Sapper answered.

"Well, let's drink to his poor little soul," Evatt proposed.

"Let's drink by all means, sir," Sapper said.

It was at this moment that Armand stepped in, feeling that the game was getting too close for comfort. He steered Sapper toward the buffet, and there they found Plato filling himself with cup after cup of bouillon, his whole face glistening and greasy.

"I can no longer stand it," Plato said in a shaking voice. "I am frightened. I cannot bear to walk around with my naked face and everyone looking at it. I am not used to it. Always behind the scenes, never in the open, that is my motto. Not a man of action—an idealist—a thinker—a dreamer—a planner of great schemes—not a man of action. I am so upset, I think I might die."

"I think so, too," Armand said, looking at him coldly.

The cup of bouillon began to shake in Plato's pudgy hand, and tears filled his eyes.

"All right, let's start," Armand said. "We will begin on the third floor, working down."

He turned to Annette.

"Please watch the orchestra," he told her. "Don't let them stop. Give us forty minutes, then meet us at the pavilion."

"*Do* try not to kill anybody, darling," she begged him. "It always leaves a mark. My bedroom is on the second floor, first to the right, in the east wing. The bag is there. I've put some of my jewelry in already."

She watched them go, the gray-coated marquis, the Franciscan friar and the jockey in his silks. She pressed her black fan against her smiling lips. She wondered what the Duchess of Alba would have done in her place: she would have found a way of keeping him forever. But she had lived in another time, when her wishes and her whims and her heart's desires could be made a law. Lady L. felt that she had been born too late. The modern world was not a place for women in love. She stopped before Goya's portrait of the divine Duchess and lifted her eyes toward her: Please help me, she prayed silently, please advise me, tell me what to do. Then, moving from group to group, talking and laughing, she was the perfect hostess again. Everything was very gay. The ball was an enormous success. Her parties always were. Her husband came to congratulate her, looking as usual very pleased with himself.

"I say, Di, a jolly good party, I call this. The best

we've given yet. By the way, Smithson has just told me
that the Ambassadorship to France is still open—he
thinks you will make a great Ambassadress. I do hope
the Queen is not going to interfere."

"I don't think she disapproves of you or me particularly," Lady L. told him. "I think she just disapproves
of Paris."

They were interrupted by a chain of dancers threading
through the rooms. Lady L. found herself surrounded by
three Italian *monsignori*—young Lord Ridgewood,
Lord Brackenfoot and Lord Chilling. They had been
trying desperately to establish a reputation for vice,
but no doubt they never got beyond drinking champagne
from a satin slipper, thought Lady L. She waved them
aside smilingly and went toward the ballroom. She sur-
reptitiously looked at the tiny enamel watch pinned to
her fichu. It was almost three o'clock now. The forty
minutes Armand had asked for were almost up. The
music had the frantic strident accents of dawn. She went
over to the Viennese conductor, a gentle, plump little
man, and asked him to keep playing for another half
hour or so. He bowed politely, without stopping the
movement of his arms. But already some of the guests
were beginning to leave, and she caught sight of Mrs.
Oulbenkian, wife of the shipping magnate, dressed as

Marie Antoinette, climbing rather wearily up the stairs.
My God, she thought, they *must* be through now!

It was then that a sudden scream sounded in the distance. Lady L. felt that it had torn the very halls apart,
but in the general laughter and noise, only she seemed
to have heard it. She walked quickly toward the marble
staircase and stood there for a moment, her head
lowered, listening, nervously playing with her fan.

Upstairs, Mrs. Oulbenkian had entered her room to
find a jockey and a Franciscan friar standing over her
open jewelcase. She had backed out screaming for help,
the piercing scream that Lady L. had heard. Armand
was then in an adjoining bedroom, and he immediately
ran out into the corridor and, signaling to the other two
to follow him, walked toward the southern wing and
down to the ground floor, where he mixed with the guests.
They could have made their exit through the southern entrance, but Plato had been holding his fear too long and
now he lost his head completely. No longer conscious
of what he was doing and still clasping the leather bag
in one hand and a diamond necklace in the other, he
flung himself headlong down the main staircase, toward
the ballroom. Even then, had he kept his wits, he could
have made his escape, for the music was still raging, the
couples whirling on the floor, and no one appeared to

have heard the scream. But instead of walking through the ballroom calmly, Plato panicked even more and, hesitating between advance and retreat, crouched against the wall with the leather bag in one hand and the diamond necklace in the other and remained there as if nailed to the ground, with his terror-stricken face for all to see. He looked so obviously like a trapped thief that even the most unsuspecting guests stopped on the dance floor and stared at him.

At that moment, the jockey, who had run after Plato and tried to stop him, appeared at the top of the stairs and Plato, looking up, saw him and began to shriek wildly, "Help! Help! They are after me!"

Sapper hesitated for one second, then backed away and vanished as the Franciscan friar was seized by Sir Allan Douglas, dressed as a conquistador, and the young Patrick O'Patrick, in a bullfighter's costume.

They had hardly reached him when Plato began to babble his confession instantly.

"I didn't want to do it, I didn't want to do it!" he started. "They made me . . ."

Lady L. pressed her hand against her throat: Plato was looking straight at her and if both his arms had not been pinioned he would have pointed at her. It was then that she saw Armand appear from among the crowd of guests and come forward slowly and calmly, a pistol in his hand. Plato saw him, too, and a feeble smile of hope began to crawl over his lips. The two men who were holding him also looked toward the strangely beautiful and romantic figure approaching them, and seeing help coming, Plato began suddenly to struggle again, trying to break free and to run toward his rescuer. Armand took one step more and, as Plato was making one more desperate effort to free himself, he lifted the pistol and shot him through the heart. There was an expression of intense surprise on the fat, round face of the Franciscan friar as he crumpled in his robe and hung limply in the hands of his captors.

"Please, ladies and gentlemen, remain calm," Armand said. "I am Captain Lagarde of the French Police. Several dangerous criminals are present here tonight, in various disguises, and I must ask you all to stay where you are. We are going to investigate the identity of every person present. My colleagues from Scotland Yard have already arrested the notorious bandit, Armand Denis. But we know that some of his accomplices are still at large. No one must leave the house under any circumstances."

The music had stopped. The guests huddled in groups, immobile and silent; it was as if a hundred escaped waxworks had suddenly returned to their stands. Armand picked up the bag at Plato's feet. He bowed to Lady L.

"Madame," he said, "I am deeply sorry that we were unable to prevent this unpleasantness. Please excuse us. It will all be over in a matter of minutes."

As he bowed again, he murmured in a barely audible voice, "I will wait for you at the pavilion." He moved away toward the terrace.

Lady L. mounted a few steps and, looking around at her guests, raised her voice a little and said, "I understand there has been a robbery but that everything will be all right. Please, Maestro, let's have some music."

There was a general murmur of excited voices, whispers and cries. Then the music began once more and the wax figures came to life again. Only the Franciscan friar was still lying motionless on the floor, his eyes open with an expression of extreme surprise.

Lady L., pulling her dress up a little, stepped around Plato and went upstairs to her room. She wondered what had happened to Sapper—but there was no time to find out. She crossed her room quickly and then, stepping through a baize-covered door leading to the servants' quarters, she reached the back staircase. It was empty, but she could hear servants running through the kitchens and corridors. Doors slammed, and there was the sound of crockery and the clatter of cutlery. In the distance, excited voices shrieked and laughed hysterically. She found herself on the cobbled pavement of the courtyard. She had hardly begun to move when she saw a shadow lying on the ground in a patch of moonlight. The jockey must have tried to climb down the water pipe from the third floor, and now he lay sprawled on the stones, his riding crop at his side, thrown for the last time. She stared at him for one brief second and then ran toward the pavilion.

CHAPTER FOURTEEN

The clouds, the moon, the stars, the night, even the shimmering leaves, all seemed to pulsate around her with each beat of her heart. The branches of lilac tore at her mantilla and she swore in French at her high-heeled shoes. She took them off and ran along the path in her stockinged feet. The clouds themselves seemed to share her panic as they fled across the sky. The moon vanished behind those shifting veils of fear as she stumbled and almost fell, swearing again. Then she was at the pavilion at last and groping in the darkness for the door.

A small candle was burning by the bed. Armand stood in the flickering light, holding the pistol in his hand. With one deep sigh, almost a sob, she flung herself against him.

"Oh, my darling, I thought you were gone."

"What happened to Sapper?"

"He's dead."

Armand said nothing, but the look of sharp pain, of a sudden and total despair, gave a tragic, haunted expression to his face, and she felt his whole body stiffen. His arms tightened around her and he held her closer, pressing his bowed head against her cheek. For one brief, unbelieving moment, a faint hope rose in her again; she closed her eyes in a fervent prayer and waited for a reassuring word, for an admission of defeat, for his voice to say at last, "I shall try no more. From now on, there will be no other cause for me but you." He remained silent; then, glancing at the little, twisted candle which seemed to be looking at them sidelong, as if tilting its head, he smiled sadly at it.

"Another comrade fallen for our cause," he said. "Sapper will not be forgotten."

He kissed her hair.

"I must go now," he said.

"Yes. You must. I know."

He kicked the bag with his foot. "There are enough jewels here to keep us going for a year."

Once more she glanced up at him with a brief, faint hope, but she knew too well what he meant by "us": millions and millions of people everywhere, from east to west, from Paris to China—so many, in fact, that they would never be able to find each other, that he would never be able to see her in the crowd.

"Yes, my darling," she told him maternally, caressing his hair.

"We will strike in Russia first, against the Czar. That is where our money will be most useful."

She was staring at him lovingly and with dislike.

"Yes, my darling," she said. "I know. I understand now."

"The little German kingdoms, like Württemberg, are also good ground for action. The students are getting restless and there will soon be barricades in the streets. But we can't be everywhere at once."

"No, of course we can't," she said. "We must do our best, though."

But he was impervious to irony—everything was

much too serious, too important, too pressing. He lacked lightness, he lacked humor; he was too earnest, too dedicated, too self-righteous in his determination to save the world. He was a selfish, egotistical, self-indulgent man who loved nothing but humanity. There was no place for her in his heart—only for mankind: he could count only in millions. He didn't know at all how to give himself, how to sacrifice himself, how to limit himself, how to love. He was disgustingly, avariciously clinging to his ideals as other greedy men cling to gold. Yet he was all she wanted. She wanted him violently, completely and ruthlessly—but she couldn't have him. She had been very unlucky. She could have loved a gambler, an opium addict, a common thief, a drunkard —but no, it had to be an idealist. Tears were forcing their way into her eyes, but she wasn't going to cry. There would be no more tears. She would say good-bye to him once more—and then she would keep him forever. She was not going to give him back to her rival, to let him go to his other and better-loved mistress. Humanity will have to fix herself up with another lover, she thought. Armand is not going back to her.

"I must go now," he said. "I have to be on the train before the police get here. That leaves me hardly an hour."

She sat on the bed and began to undress. She stared defiantly at him while she undressed, without a word. She was half naked soon, still staring at him, sitting on the bed, her breasts bare, the black mantilla with the red tulle rose still in her hair. She now knew what the Duchess of Alba would have done in her place, and she was going to do it. She hated her rival too much. He was not going back to his millions.

"Darling," he said, smiling hesitantly, "there is so little time—"

"You cannot go now," she told him. "It's much too dangerous. You will be safe here for a couple of days. It is my private retreat and no one is ever allowed to come here. I have the only key. Then, when things quiet down, you will go. . . . You will go back to your other and greater love."

The twisted candle flickered and shadows were trembling on the wall. The pink dress of the Duchess of Alba was flowing to her feet. Armand leaned over her and kissed her shoulder.

"I think you are right. It's a much better plan. Your head is much cooler than mine. You must always be with me to help me."

Her voice shook a little as she said lovingly, "Yes, my darling, I'll help you."

She put her arms around his neck and pulled him toward her and fell back with his mouth against hers. Tears were streaming from her eyes as she felt his lips, caressed his hair, and knew for the last time her happiness as a woman. Tears kept running faster and faster down her cheeks, and in the end she didn't even know if her sobs were the voice of despair or the last parting words of happiness that would never be again.

She sighed deeply and began to dress again. Armand was lying on his back, his eyes half closed, as if he were waiting for his body to return. She didn't dare look at him. She was determined, but she was not going to take chances with herself. It had to be done now, quickly and forever, so that there would never be any more partings.

"I must go now. I will keep the key. No one will look for you here. I will be back in the morning, as soon as the police have gone."

He was playing with her mantilla and the rose that had fallen from her hair. She put her shoes on and opened the door. She stepped out into the graying night and then, with a gasp, pulled back.

"Armand, quick, they are coming!"

He jumped to his feet. She saw that he was looking

for his pistol and she rushed to him and grabbed him
by the hand.

"No, no, please—hide here. Quickly."

She turned the key in the lock of the Madras strongbox and opened it.

"Please, my darling, quick! They won't find you
here. . . ."

He stepped inside, still holding the mantilla and the
rose. She looked around, then grabbed the bag with the
jewels and the pistol and threw them inside. Then she
smiled at him for the last time, a tender and cruel smile.

"They will soon be gone. We will never part again."

She closed the door and turned the heavy key twice
in the lock.

Sir Percy Rodiner sat in his chair, very erect, his
face a ghastly white, breathing noisily and very fast,
as if he had been running. He tried to get up, to speak,
and began to raise his hand, but his hand fell down
helplessly again. Lady L. stood in front of the Madras
strongbox, looking at it with a tender, cruel smile—the
famous smile of Lady L.

She was speaking.

"My poor darling," she was saying. "You were so
very, very cruel to me—and I loved you so much. I only

wish you knew that your son is the present Duke of Glendale, all your grandchildren pillars of society. James is Director of the Bank of England, Anthony will soon be a bishop, Richard is in the Guards, and Roland is a Cabinet Minister—all good Conservatives, all of them. That ought to teach you."

The Poet Laureate managed this time to raise his hand. It was shaking. But he did succeed in pointing a finger at the heavy, squat thing that stood there like a one-man fortress.

Lady L. was speaking again.

"Sometimes I cannot bear it," she said. "I just can't bear the idea that one day I will die and lose you forever. I just can't imagine not coming here to be with you, to sit with you, to talk to you, to live with you as I have done almost every day during the last sixty years."

The Poet Laureate finally managed to speak. But his voice came out strangely high and almost eunuchlike, and even then he couldn't find the words.

"You mean to say that he's still—that you have . . ."

Then his voice failed him again and he just sat there, pointing a shaking finger at the thing.

Lady L. took from her pocket a heavy black key and

put it into the lock. She turned it twice and opened the door.

Armand was kneeling there in his gray courtier coat. The white knee breeches and the silk stockings adhered to the bones, or hung limply around them. There was a leather bag—with a black mantilla over it. A pistol lay between the buckled shoes. The right hand of the skeleton held a red tulle rose.

ABOUT THE AUTHOR

ROMAIN GARY *has had three careers: as writer, soldier and diplomat. His first novel,* Education Européenne, *won the Prix des Critiques in 1945 and was a sensational best seller throughout Europe.* The Roots of Heaven, *his fifth novel, won him the highest French literary honor— the Prix Goncourt—and sold 300,000 copies in France, then went on to become a tremendous critical and popular success in England and America.*

M. Gary began his military career in 1937, when he enlisted in the French Air Force. He served in France until it fell to Hitler, then joined the R.A.F. and finally fought with the Free French. He received the Croix de la Libération, the Croix de Guerre, and was made a Chevalier of the Légion d'Honneur.

He is now a career diplomat and has served France in her embassies in England, Bulgaria and Switzerland, and as First Secretary of the French delegation to the United Nations. At present he is French Consul-General in Los Angeles. He was born in 1914, received a law degree, speaks and writes English, Russian and Polish in addition to French. He is married to the English writer, Lesley Blanch.